His kiss had changed everything

"You're looking for a wife—you said so. But I don't want to be anyone's wife. So we're certainly not going to get sexually involved just because we live in the same house," Clem ranted, glaring at him. "How long since you've been with a woman, Josh?"

"Too long, obviously," he snapped, wanting to shake her, wanting to kiss her again, wanting to touch her so badly that he ached with the need, then hating himself—and her—for this need.

She looked, if anything, relieved by his response. "It's not really me, then," she said. "Anyone would do."

He was damned if she was going to get away with that. "Don't be naive!"

SANDRA FIELD

Safety in Numbers

Harlequin Books

TORONTO • NEW YORK • LONDON
AMSTERDAM • PARIS • SYDNEY • HAMBURG
STOCKHOLM • ATHENS • TOKYO • MILAN
MADRID • WARSAW • BUDAPEST • AUCKLAND

Harlequin Presents first edition November 1992
ISBN 0-373-11506-7

Original hardcover edition published in 1991
by Mills & Boon Limited

SAFETY IN NUMBERS

CHAPTER ONE

THE two men standing face-to-face near the crowded security gate at the airport would not have been taken for father and son.

Graham MacNeill was in his early sixties, an ordinary-looking gray-haired man who brought the word "decent" instantly to mind, for his mild blue eyes combined tolerance and intelligence. Rather than standing out in the crowd, he blended with it.

His son Joshua, taller by four inches, younger by thirty years, also had blue eyes. But his were a deeper blue, as changeable as the depths of the ocean, as restless as its surface. While the father looked tired, the son looked exhausted, as though he had suffered under a terrible strain for far too long and had come too close to his breaking point for his own comfort. His belted beige trench coat showed the width of his shoulders without revealing how much weight he had lost; his face was lined as it had not been a year ago, and there were threads of gray in the well-cut dark hair that brushed his ears. He certainly did not look ordinary, nor did he blend with the crowd. Of the several women waiting to go through security a good proportion gave him a second glance, and some a third; he was one of those men who defined masculinity, all the more effectively because one suspected he was quite unconscious of his power.

The furthest thing from Josh's mind right now was his effect on the opposite sex. He said to his father, "You're sure you're ready to go back to Vancouver? I know it's home now...but you're welcome to stay here with me if you want to."

Graham cleared his throat and said bluffly, "You've had me around long enough. What's it been, two and a half months? Time I left you to your own devices."

"I don't feel that way, Dad," Josh replied with sudden intensity. "You saved my life—you know that as well as I do."

"Now, Josh, there's no need to go into that."

Josh rested his hands on the shoulders of his father's expensive cashmere overcoat. "I'll only say this once. But it needs to be said. I can never repay you for all you've done the last few months. I'd still be in that——" his mind automatically censored the words he had been going to use and substituted evenly "—prison if you hadn't raised heaven and earth to find me. And I'd probably have been six feet under in the first week I was free if you hadn't just about hijacked that government jet to get me to London. You did save my life, Dad." His voice roughened with emotion. "To say thanks sounds pitifully inadequate, doesn't it? Nevertheless, that's what I'm saying."

He put his arms around his father and hugged him with something of the same awkwardness as his speech. His father was, despite the expensive overcoat, less substantial than he had expected, and he felt a pang of love, painful and fierce and very new. Before he could lose his courage he added, "I neglected you for years—I don't deserve all you've done for me."

Graham smoothed down his hair with a hand that was not quite steady. "You're my son," he said. "I'd do it again tomorrow. And I was just as guilty of the neglect."

Josh managed a grin, trying to relieve the tension. "I did tend to be in out-of-the-way places."

"The deserts of Persia. The rain forests of Papua New Guinea. And then Africa."

Josh's face shadowed. "Yeah ... Africa."

Graham said urgently, "Look after yourself, won't you, Josh? I wish you'd come home with me—you could stay as long as you needed. Recuperate at your own speed."

"I don't know why I've got this compulsion to stay here in Halifax," Josh admitted. "I know I grew up here, and for twenty years it was home. But that was a long time ago...I'm sure most of my friends have left for the bright lights of Toronto by now. Or Vancouver." He hesitated, wondering if his father would tell him to mind his own business. "Does Halifax still hold bad memories for you?"

Graham appeared to be absorbed in a young couple exchanging a passionate embrace not twenty feet away. "You could say so...I never really got over Arabella, Josh. I know you didn't like her—but she's the reason I haven't remarried. Had no desire to."

Arabella had been Josh's stepmother for two short years; Arabella had been the cause of his parents' divorce, and had divorced her own husband to marry Graham. "No, I never liked her. But I was only fifteen at the time."

"She's the one who kept us apart, though. Even after she left."

Josh, an honest man, could not deny this. "I'm sorry about that—we wasted a lot of years. Do you have any idea what happened to her? Where she is?"

"None. I've thought of having her traced...but what's the point? I'm sixty-two, Josh, and I'm sure she's happily married."

"I don't imagine my attitude helped at the time."

Graham smiled wryly. "Oh, her daughter hated me as much as you hated Arabella." He shrugged his shoulders and went on with a deliberate lightening of his tone, "Talking of being happily married, maybe it's about time you tried it—I wouldn't mind becoming a grandfather one of these days. You could give that some thought, hmm?"

It was Josh's turn to give a wry smile. "I thought about it quite a lot while I was in that hellhole—the one thing I had there was time to think. I'm ready to settle down now, Dad, put down some roots. And I guess that includes marriage. Only thing is, I don't have anyone in mind."

"You won't find her until you start looking." Graham slapped his son on the arm and glanced down at his boarding pass. "I should go through security; they'll be boarding in five minutes. Call me any time, Josh, day or night, and come for a visit whenever you feel like it."

"I will. Don't work too hard." The words were a cover, Josh knew, for a depth of emotion with which each of them was still shy. They hugged again, then Graham picked up his leather briefcase and headed for the gateway. The attendant checked his boarding pass and with a last salute of his hand Graham disappeared from sight.

Josh picked up his suitcase, which contained a minimal number of belongings, all of them new, and started down the hallway to the taxi stand at the far end of the terminal. He'd already booked a room in a downtown hotel. Once he was settled in, he'd start looking for an apartment.

And maybe along the way he'd figure out what he was doing in Halifax... why he had had this strange compulsion to come back to the city where he had been born.

*   *   *

The house was perfect.

Josh stood by the gate, the chill April wind swirling the dirt in the gutter and knifing through his trench coat; he'd forgotten the vicissitudes of spring on Canada's eastern coast, and forgotten too the edge to which the cold Atlantic could hone the wind. He'd spent too long in the tropics.

But the garden that surrounded the house was sheltered by a hedge and a section of rather rickety fence, and only the top branches of the pine and maple trees were tossing in the breeze. Although snow, grimy and frozen, still lay against the north wall of the house, it had long since thawed on the south side, and clusters of tiny crocuses, purple and gold, intermingled with snowdrops, were blooming beneath the shrubs. Birds chittered around the feeders suspended near a tangle of rosebushes, and he could imagine himself sitting in the sun on the worn concrete bench nearby.

The house was Victorian, tall and many-gabled with three chimneys set in the green-shingled roof, and, like the garden, it needed work. But the setting sun twinkled a welcome on the windowpanes and gilded the wicker chairs sitting patiently on the front porch waiting for summer, while the brass lantern and number plate to one side of the door were freshly polished.

I want to live here, Josh thought, and beneath his tiredness felt a surge of longing. It's been waiting for me, this house. It knew I was coming.

He must be tired, he thought ruefully, for he was not normally a fanciful man. He'd had no time for that. He pushed open the gate, which swung smoothly on well-oiled hinges, and walked up the path. It was fifteen minutes past six, and the advertisement for this particular house had said to call after six. He only hoped no one had got here before him.

The porch steps needed painting. Conquering a strong urge to peek through the long-paned windows, he pushed the doorbell and heard it peal inside. There had been no lights on in the house; maybe he was too early.

He waited a few moments before pushing the bell again. Then his head turned. Footsteps were coming down the street toward the house, and—the sound carried on the wind—someone was singing. A woman.

Josh saw her before she saw him. She was tall, with a mane of tangled brown hair, her stride full of energy; it was she who was singing, although with more enthusiasm than trueness of pitch. Nevertheless, with a quiver of inner amusement he recognized the conquering hero chorus from Handel's *Judas Maccabaeus*. Somehow he was not at all surprised when she pushed on the gate.

Then she saw him and stopped dead.

With quick compunction he realized what she would be seeing: a large unknown male standing on her front porch at twilight. He called out, "I've come to see about the upstairs apartment . . . the ad said six o'clock."

"Oh." She closed the gate and walked more slowly up the path. Her raincoat was of some shiny red fabric with a generous Paisley scarf draped over the collar; because he was facing the sun, her face was in shadow. She said politely, stopping at the bottom of the steps, "I'm afraid you've come for nothing—I only rent to women."

His eyes narrowed. "I beg your pardon?"

"I only rent to women," she repeated. "I always put it in the ad—but this time I forgot."

Josh had been half prepared to be told that the apartment was already rented. But nothing would have prepared him to find out that he could not have it because he was a man. Not altogether convinced she was serious, he said, "Why don't we at least go inside where we can discuss this?"

"There's nothing to discuss." She climbed the steps, standing only a couple of feet away from him. "I'm truly sorry if I've caused you any inconvenience...I must give the paper a call and change the ad before it goes in tomorrow."

"So you haven't found anyone?" he flashed.

"People could be trying to get hold of me by phone right now. So if you'll excuse me?"

She was searching in her handbag for her key. Josh stood very still. He wasn't quite sure how he was going to handle this situation, but he was absolutely sure of one thing: he was not going to walk meekly down the steps and away from this wonderful house. Just because he wasn't a woman.

A quick scrutiny of her face—and he was a man used to assessing people—told him that she was not about to change her mind. She'd meant every word when she'd said there was nothing to discuss. We'll see about that, he thought, and said calmly, "The name's MacNeill. Because I love what I've seen of the garden and of the outside of the house, I'm prepared to take the apartment sight unseen. Which will save you the cost of another ad."

She had found the key. Looking at him unsmilingly from gray eyes as cool as rain, she said, "I've paid for three days. I don't rent to men. Good evening, Mr. MacNeill."

She turned away, inserting the key and pushed the door open. Moving swiftly for a man who had recently been extremely ill, Josh pushed himself through the open door, narrowly avoided collision with the back of her shiny red raincoat and stationed himself three or four feet away from her, leaving the door agape. He said a little breath-

lessly, his eyes laughing at her, "Don't be frightened—
the door stays open and you can leave any time. I
just——"

"Do I look frightened?"

Not frightened. Furious. Josh said trenchantly, "No.
Which makes you not very smart—considering I could
be a potential murderer, rapist or thief. As it happens
I'm none of the above. Merely a potential tenant who's
damned if he's going to be sent away hat in hand because he's the wrong sex."

She marched to the door and slammed it shut. "I can't
afford to heat the front porch," she said, glaring at him.
"Now, Mr. MacNeill, you listen to me——"

"I'll pay you double whatever you're asking. I'll paint
the front steps. I'll weed the garden. The only thing I
won't do is wear a skirt."

With an angry snap of her fingers she flipped on the
nearest light switch. Josh added spontaneously, "What
a magnificent staircase!"

"I did not invite you into my house to admire the
staircase. I didn't invite you at all. Will you please leave
immediately?"

Josh dragged his eyes away from the gracious curve
of what looked like mahogany railings. He could have
said that she looked magnificent, too. Although it would
have been the truth, he didn't think it would be a wise
move, for her eyes, no longer a cool gray, were as turbulent as storm clouds and she did not look in any mood
to be receptive to compliments. "No," he said.

"Then I'll call the police."

"Go ahead," he said mildly. "I can tell them how
you're restricting your apartment to women. I'm sure
the Landlord and Tenancy Act must have a clause pro-
hibiting discrimination on the basis of sex. Or else the

Human Rights Act does. It'll be interesting to see what the lawyers say."

She had started across the hall to the telephone. Whirling in a flare of red plastic, she spat, "I've had women for the last five years! And nobody's complained."

"What have you got against men?"

"Nothing! As you can see from where you're standing, the upstairs and the downstairs of this house aren't truly separate. So I feel more comfortable renting to another woman rather than to a man."

"Privacy is very high on my list," Josh said. "You can be sure I'd respect yours. So I can't imagine that the layout of the house would be any problem."

"You know," she said sweetly, "you really have a nerve. You offer me twice the rent without even knowing how much I'm asking, you push your way in here like a common thief, and then, just to top that, you threaten to set the law on me. You will forgive me if you don't seem quite the ideal tenant."

Feeling more alive than he had for days, Josh gave her a lazy grin. "That's where you're wrong. I can give you letters of reference, a credit rating and postdated checks. I don't smoke and I've outgrown wild parties. What more do you want?"

"A soprano voice, perhaps?"

He laughed, he who had wondered more than once in the last six months if he would ever laugh again. "I'm a baritone who sings off-key—some things in life are immutable. But I like Handel's oratorios."

There was an unmistakable flare of interest in her eyes, which just as quickly she extinguished. "*I* like renting to women," she said stubbornly. "You'd be a nuisance. I couldn't wander around in my underwear."

"Neither, in the interests of equality, could I."

"I don't——" She broke off as the telephone shrilled from a room behind her. "Excuse me."

Josh stared at her retreating back. It would be a woman on the line, he thought, and he would lose his chance to live in a house that instinctively he knew would help him to heal. As a wave of exhaustion washed over him, he leaned back against the wall, hearing the sudden shallowness of his breathing, cursing the weakness of his knees. A natural side effect, the doctor in London had said, of these debilitating attacks of fatigue. Nothing to worry about. They would pass as he got his strength back.

He closed his eyes. The house creaked in the wind. A cat mewed over the low murmur of the woman's voice. He hadn't even found out her name. He was losing his touch...

"Are you all right?"

His eyes flew open and he pushed himself away from the wall. He knew from looking in the mirror in the hotel room how the light above his head must be delineating the sallowness of his skin and the dark circles under his eyes, and with all his remaining energy he repelled any sympathy she might be tempted to offer. "I've been ill," he said. "Did you rent it to her?"

"She's allergic to cats. Of which I have two. Are you allergic to cats, Mr. MacNeill?"

There was mockery in her eyes rather than sympathy. Josh glanced down at her ankles—admirable ankles—where an immense black cat was fawning over her trim brown loafers. "No."

"You look awful," she said.

He looked at her warily; her statement sounded detached and not at all sympathetic. He said, deciding that a partial version of the truth might serve him best, "I've been in the tropics, where I got malaria. But I doubt if there'll be any recurrence, and if there should be I have all the drugs I'd need—I'd be no trouble to you."

"Are you employed?"

She had, he supposed, a perfect right to ask that question. And at least she wasn't showing him the door. "I'm still on sick leave. In three months I have to decide whether I want to go back to the oil company I've been with as a lawyer for the last ten years... they'll give you the references I mentioned. The alternative is to free-lance, start up something on my own." Suddenly tired of all this verbal fencing, he added impatiently, "Look, I'll sign a lease for three months but I'll give you checks for six. If I leave midsummer, you'll have the rent covered until the fall, and you shouldn't have any trouble renting your apartment when the students come back to university. Take it or leave it."

With another of those cool, considering looks she said, "You're a very stubborn man—in the pink of health you'd be a force to be reckoned with. Do you want to see the apartment?"

"Do you mean you'll rent it to me?"

"You might hate it," she said.

"If I'm stubborn, you're aggravating!"

She laughed. "You're not the first man to tell me that. Which reminds me, we'd better hurry; I have a date at seven-thirty."

She flung her raincoat casually over the newel post, revealing a gray corduroy skirt and a multicolored bulky sweater, and started up the stairs. She had very long legs. Studiously keeping his eyes on the threadbare pattern of the carpet, Josh followed her, and heard the patter of paws as the black cat trotted after him.

The apartment had a living room with a brick fireplace, an adequate bathroom, a tiny kitchen with a balcony, and a bedroom that overlooked the street. The color schemes were soft, and while none of the furnishings were expensive they had been chosen with care and lovingly painted. Everything was spotlessly clean. He said, frowning, "This isn't the whole upstairs of the house, is it?"

"No." She indicated a door off the hall. "There's another wing through there that I can't afford to fix up." She added abruptly, "When you frown like that, you remind me of someone. But I can't think who."

They were standing by the fireplace, in the warm glow of a little lamp set in the wall. "I only arrived here two days ago," Josh said. "I've never seen you before...I would have remembered you, I'm sure."

"For my singing," she said flippantly.

"What else?" he parried, and found himself wondering with whom she had a date. He would have remembered her for more than her singing, he knew; her eyes alone were hauntingly beautiful, well worth remembering. The rest of her face, feature by feature, could not quite account for the impression she gave of intelligence allied with humor, of physical grace married to inner strength. She was a woman who knew herself, he thought slowly. And, more rare, liked what she knew.

She raised her chin. "That was a very comprehensive survey."

"I'm sorry—I didn't mean to stare."

"The rent's six hundred a month, including heat and lights. You pay your own telephone. And I won't take a cent more than that, so you can forget your idea of paying me double."

Oddly enough the belligerent tilt of her chin did stir some long-dead memory. Quite unable to pin it down to either a person or a place, Josh said, "You really mean that, don't you? Yet obviously you could use the money."

"Six hundred a month."

So she had her pride, this tall young woman with the mop of toffee-colored curls and the level gray eyes. "Everything I mentioned—references, checks and so on—can be ready by noon tomorrow," he said. "If I dropped them off where you work, you could look them over, and then I could come here at six to see what you've decided."

"And what if the answer's no?" she said evenly.

"Don't ask me to explain why I want to live here so badly I can taste it—I don't know why!" Josh burst out, annoyed as much with himself as with her. "It's certainly not like me to be so damned irrational. If you say no, Miss—I don't even know your name, for heaven's sake!"

"Clem Delaney. Ms."

He went on more calmly, "If you say no, Ms. Delaney, I promise I'll leave without making a fuss, and I won't come back."

She held out her hand. "Fine."

He shook it, liking the smoothness of her palm and the strength of her grip, pleased that she had so forthrightly accepted his word. "Where do you work?"

"The Mother Goose Daycare Center, on Leyton Street . . . off East Avenue."

"I'll be there by noon."

She glanced at her watch and said with comical dismay, "I've got to get supper, have a shower and feed the cats—all in forty-five minutes."

Josh led the way out of the room, managed not to trip over the black cat, who had sprawled himself across the lintel, and ran down the stairs. She said, "There's a downtown bus at the end of the street in ten minutes; if you hurry you can catch it. Goodbye, Mr. MacNeill."

Her mind was very clearly on all she had to do rather than on him. He said dryly, "Goodbye, Ms. Delaney," and let himself out. The wind had died but the temperature had dropped. He pulled up his collar and set off for the bus.

The Mother Goose Daycare Center was painted a cheerful yellow, its sign lettered in green, red and blue with a border of flowers. Standing on the pavement outside it, conducting what looked like a very spirited argument with a man leaning against a lamppost, was Ms. Clem Delaney.

Josh stopped on the corner. She was wearing the same corduroy skirt and bulky sweater, her hands thrust in her pockets; it was too cold for her to be without a coat, he thought, and transferred his attention to the young man.

He disliked him on sight, from his slicked-back black hair and his black leather jacket to his too-tight black jeans and high black leather boots. No chains. No skull and crossbones on the back of the jacket. No motorbike. For those lacks Josh gave thanks, although they did not cause his dislike to lessen. He moved a little closer, shamelessly eavesdropping.

"—saw you last night at *Born on the Fourth of July*," the young man was saying. "How come you'll date that jerk and you won't date me?"

"Brad, I can choose who I go out with—I have that right."

"Okay, okay. So I'll pick you up after work and we'll go get a bite to eat."

"I can't, I'm busy."

With a sinuous grace that reminded Josh of snakes, Brad abandoned the lamppost and moved closer to Clem. "Who is it tonight?" he demanded.

"I told you the day we met that I don't want to settle down and I like dating different men. If you didn't like that, you didn't have to go with me. That was two weeks ago, and I haven't changed my mind."

"I'm not into sharing."

"You're talking as though you have some kind of claim on me," Clem snorted. "You don't! And I won't date anyone who puts constraints on me."

"You're crazy, you know that?" Brad said unpleasantly.

"Then why do you want to date me?" was Clem's impatient, if less than diplomatic response. "Brad, I've got to go inside, I'm freezing."

But Brad grabbed her by the arm, yanking her toward him, his light blue eyes suddenly empty of expression. "You're——"

Josh said politely, "Hello, Clem. I brought you the papers you wanted."

Brad's head jerked around and in basic Anglo-Saxon he told Josh where to go. Josh, who from the age of four had never been one to back down from a fight, balanced himself lightly on the balls of his feet and said, "Let go of her arm."

But Clem pulled her own arm free and hissed at Josh with a noticeable lack of gratitude, "I can look after myself! You're making a scene outside the place where I work and I'm in much greater danger of catching pneumonia than I am from Brad. You can give me the papers now, and Brad, don't you come here again."

She extracted the long white envelope from Josh's fingers, scowled at them both impartially and took the yellow-painted steps two at a time. The door of the Mother Goose Daycare Center closed behind her.

Methodically Brad went through a somewhat limited list of epithets. Focusing his light blue eyes on Josh, he added, "You stay outa my way, buddy." He then loped across the road and vanished down a side street. Josh gave a philosophical shrug of his shoulders and went in search of a salad bar for lunch. As he munched his way through a generous if rather limp Caesar salad, he cogitated on what he had learned today about Ms. Clem Delaney.

If Brad was anything to go by, she was a poor judge of men.

She did not appreciate being rescued.

And she had a fiery temper. Although he had already known that.

He speared an anchovy that looked as if it had been recycled. Also she owned a house she could not afford and a garden that was too big for her. And he had five hours to wait before he found out whether he was going to be living in that house or not.

Promptly at six Josh presented himself at the front door of the old house on Weymouth Street. There was a light shining in the hall; Clem was home. He schooled his face to a confidence he was far from feeling and pressed the doorbell.

Clem whipped the door open, gestured for him to enter and closed it sharply behind him. She did not offer to take his coat. Instead she demanded, "You don't recognize me, do you? You don't have a clue who I am!"

Her tone was distinctly unfriendly and it was not a reception he could have anticipated. But Josh was used to facing boards of directors who wanted hard facts and accountants who wanted hard cash, and consequently was not easily fazed. He loosened the belt of his raincoat, gave her flushed face a leisurely survey, and drawled, "Can't say I do."

"Why didn't you tell me your name was Joshua?"

"You didn't ask. Is it important?"

"My name's Clementina. Tina Linton, I was, before your father married my mother."

Josh felt his jaw drop. "You're *Arabella's* daughter? Good God."

"Yes. I'm Arabella's daughter. I hated your guts when I was ten years old."

Still grappling with her new identity, Josh said, "It looks as if you still do."

"You're the one who told me what was going on—that your father was having an affair with my mother. Or don't you remember that, either?"

She was breathing hard through her nostrils and her breasts under the multicolored sweater were heaving up and down in a way Josh tried his best to ignore. He said blankly and with a total lack of tact, "You can't be Tina. You're beautiful!"

"Thanks a lot," she snarled.

He ran his fingers through his hair, trying to collect his wits. "I didn't mean——"

"Oh, yes, you did."

Her anger ignited his own. "All right, so I did," Josh said. "Tina Linton was a skinny little thing with braces on her teeth and glasses on her nose, who never spoke one civil word to me . . . do you wonder that I didn't recognize her? After all, *you* didn't recognize *me*."

"That last time I saw you, you had an Apache haircut with sideburns dyed burgundy and you were trying to grow a moustache. Plus you used to dress like Brad—don't you *dare* laugh at me!"

For Josh was laughing, a helpless belly laugh that took him back in time and made him feel twenty years younger. "I wore jeans so tight I could hardly sit down," he choked, "and copper bracelets—you left out the bracelets. I thought my father was going to have apoplexy when I went home with that haircut."

He wiped his eyes, laughter still trembling in his chest. "That's no doubt why I reacted as I did to Brad—an earlier incarnation right there on the sidewalk." He sobered. "Watch out for that guy, Clem—I'll have to call you Clem, you're just not Tina to me at all—he's bad news."

"I was not aware that I had asked you for advice," she replied with dangerous quietness. "Nor will you have to call me anything. If you think I'm going to let you live in my house, you can think again!"

Josh was visited with the mad urge to pull her into his arms and kiss her very thoroughly; he then tried to rationalize the urge by telling himself what a long time it had been since he had kissed a woman. Any woman. Stifling the urge—for it would surely sabotage any hope of ever living in this house—and hoping it had not shown in his face, he said, "Look, why don't we go out for a drink and a bite to eat? We've got a lot to talk about."

"I can't. I already have a date."

"Another movie?" he ventured.

"Douglas is coming over to study for his exams."

Almost certain what answer he was going to get, Josh asked, "And what did Douglas think of *Born on the Fourth of July*?"

"I went to the movies with Jamie."

"You play the field."

"Safety in numbers," she said. "You're changing the subject."

He looked at her in silence. "I should have recognized you," he said slowly. "Because one thing hasn't changed—your eyes always were beautiful."

She crossed her arms over her chest. "Don't substitute flattery for truth, Joshua...what really hasn't changed is my temper."

The urge to kiss her revisited him; he slapped it down. Holding her eyes with his, he said quietly, "I was telling the truth."

"Oh." Her lashes fluttered down. "Then I guess I shouldn't have said that."

"You have every right to be angry with me," Josh admitted, knowing the words had to be said, and were indeed long overdue. He swallowed. "I've owed you an apology for a good many years. I haven't forgotten that I'm the one who told you that my father and your mother were having an affair—nor have I forgotten how brutally I did so. I was so full of hurt and confusion that I lashed out at you, dumping it all on you so I wouldn't have to deal with it. I'll always remember your face when I told you—you looked...stricken. And you were only ten years old. I was fifteen, and five years means a lot at that age. Ever since then I've felt guilty about the way I treated you." He bit his lip. "I'm sorry. Easy to say, I know—but I really mean it."

She blinked, her eyes suddenly swimming in tears. He said savagely, "There were a lot of tears shed then, weren't there? You. My mother. I would have shed a few of my own if I hadn't figured my manhood would have been on the line."

Clem fished in her pocket for a Kleenex, blew her nose, and said defiantly, "It wasn't all my mother's fault."

"Is that what I said to you back then? I'm really sorry, Clem...of course it wasn't. I'm not sure it was anyone's fault."

She let out her breath in a long sigh, her shoulders sagging. "For a long time I blamed your father. But I suppose you're right—no one was really to blame."

"One of those times in my life when I did a lot of growing up," he said wryly. "Was it like that for you?"

Her lips twisted. "That came later—when my mother left your father and remarried."

"Someone called Delaney."

"No. Andy Fougere was her third husband. Eric Delaney was her fourth."

Her voice had sunk to a whisper, so that Josh could barely hear her, and he felt his heart clench with a pity he knew better than to express. He was also gaining an inkling why it was Jamie one night and Douglas the next, with someone like Brad thrown in for good measure. "Is she still married to him?"

Clem shook her head. "She's on her own right now. Has been for four years."

The light shone on her down-bent head, glinting in her tumbled curls. Josh said strongly, "I'd really like to live here, Clem. I've had a lot of...difficulties the last while, and I need to put the pieces back together. Once I've done that, got my energy back, I'll move on and get out of your hair."

She looked him full in the face. "I'd made up my mind before you came that I wouldn't let you live here."

"I know." He struggled to find the words that would say what he meant, no more and no less. "I want to stay here for myself, no point in pretending otherwise. But now there's more to it than that—I'd like to make amends, if I could. I'm not going to be working for the next few weeks. I could putter around the house, do some painting, dig in the garden—if you'd let me. Perhaps that might negate some of the hurt and anger we went through all those years ago...do you understand what I mean or do you think I'm out of my head?"

It took her a few moments to speak, moments that seemed to Josh to stretch out for a very long time; his heart was beating so loudly that he was sure she must be able to hear it. Then her face changed, opening to him like a flower to the sun, her mouth curving in a smile he had never seen before, a smile that disarmed him. She said, "I know exactly what you mean. I think it's a good idea."

He said huskily, "You're very generous, Clem."

As though she was frightened by the emotion in his voice, she said airily, "Not that generous—it's going to cost you six hundred dollars a month for the privilege of painting my dining room."

Afraid she might change her mind, he asked, "Can I move in tomorrow? Everything I own is in one suitcase, so it won't take long." The rest of his belongings had gone up in flames when the guerrillas had burned the compound.

"I'll give you a key, then you can come and go as you please." With obvious relief she chattered on about business matters, then described the vagaries of the hot water tank and the furnace. "If I'm in the shower you can't run the hot water upstairs, and vice versa, and I'd appreciate it if you'd turn the heat down at night. And if you ever lose your key, there's a spare set in the kitchen." She frowned. "I don't think there are any other house rules."

With a deadpan expression on his face Josh said, "No wandering around in our underwear. You forgot that one."

Her lashes flickered. "I just hope I'm doing the right thing," she muttered. "Maybe Brad was right—I *am* crazy."

The key was in his hand; she couldn't change her mind. "You can get rid of me in three months," Josh comforted her.

"In some ways you haven't changed at all," she said darkly. "I'll cash your checks at the first of every month."

"Fine," he said, and decided that tonight he was going to leave before she pushed him out. "I'll probably get here around noon tomorrow. Good night."

He left her standing in the hallway with the air of a woman who had radically changed her mind and was not quite sure how this has come about. He was whistling as he latched the gate behind him, and the tune he had chosen was "See, The Conqu'ring Hero Comes."

CHAPTER TWO

A WEEK passed. If Josh had been asked how the move into the old house on Weymouth Street was affecting him, the word "sleep" would have been the first to come to mind. Every night in the big brass bed under the eaves he was sleeping deeply and dreamlessly, sleeping as he had not slept since that monstrous day in the clearing when he had found the bodies of his friends...

Because he was sleeping so well, his energy was coming back, and not until it started to return did he fully realize how frightened he'd been that he would be left forever with that deadweight of exhaustion pressing his body into the ground. Each morning now he woke with a sense of anticipation for the day ahead; and the surges of fatigue that made him grab at the nearest wall for support came less and less frequently.

His first day in the apartment he took a cab and bought sheets, towels and a minimum of groceries; the next day he stocked the kitchen cupboards and started buying plants and clothes. On the third day he bought a car, a sporty red car that it gave him immense pleasure to park in Clem's driveway, and on the fourth he bought a television set and two paintings: a snowbound landscape for the living room and a seascape for his bedroom.

The old house enfolded him; as he had known it would, it gave him peace.

However, it gave him very little of Clem's company.

In a house where he shared the front door and the hallway with her, he saw astonishingly little of her, and when he did see her she managed to combine casual

27

friendliness with the unmistakable message that this
friendliness had definite limits beyond which he'd better
not trespass. He saw more of her boyfriends than he did
of her.

He met Jamie the day he bought the plants. Jamie
was a university football coach with a handsome if rather
stolid face, who carried a six-foot potted palm up the
stairs as if it were an African violet. Two days later
Douglas found the hammer for him when Josh arrived
home with the paintings, and helped him hang them;
Josh liked Douglas, who apart from being rail-thin must
have been at least two inches shorter than Clem and was
entirely comfortable with that fact. On Saturday, from
the bedroom window, Josh watched Clem get into a beige
Mercedes escorted by a new man, a man he instantly
labeled dull; Clem was wearing a dashing green cloak
with her hair piled on top of her head and looked very
beautiful. Josh cooked his own supper and watched television and did not hear her come home.

In his first week in the house he also got acquainted
with the cats. The large black cat, who liked to station
himself where someone would be sure to trip over him,
was called Armand; Rosebud was an aloof tabby with
a tendency to hold her nose in the air whenever she saw
Josh. Josh liked cats. But they could hardly be con-
sidered a substitute for Clem's company.

On Sunday, feeling oddly restless even though he had
a good book to read by the fire, Josh phoned his father.
He described the improvement in his health and his
pleasure in the apartment, then said deliberately, "You'll
never guess who my landlady is…Arabella's daughter."

Several seconds of expensive silence hummed along
the wires. "You're not serious?" Graham croaked.

Giving his father time to recover, Josh described how
he and Clem had not recognized each other. "Arabella

married twice after you and she divorced," he added. "But she's on her own now—her name's Delaney."

"Where is she?"

"I don't know. But I can find out."

"Call me back as soon as you know!"

No hesitation there. Josh said thoughtfully, "You're sure about that?"

"Of course I'm sure—I'm not a child, Josh."

"Even though she's not married, she might be involved with someone else."

"If she is, I'll give him a damned good run for his money," said Graham. "Or poke him in the nose."

"I see," said Josh, glad his father couldn't see the expression on his face. "I'll ask Clem, and I'll get back to you. It might take a couple of days—I don't see that much of her."

"Make the opportunity, Josh. This is important!"

"I'll do it as soon as I can catch her between her job and her men friends," Josh replied, sounding more exasperated than he cared for.

"Ah...so she's like Arabella."

"No. Not really." Josh scowled into the phone. "She's beautiful, as was Arabella, of course, but in a very different way. Arabella went in for frills and floppy hats, an overt kind of femininity...Clem's every bit as feminine, but—hell, Dad, I don't know how to describe her. She's independent. She's capable. She's assertive." He ran his fingers through his hair. "She's got a temper."

"She had that when she was ten years old," Graham said dryly. "Are you planning to become one of the men friends?"

"I don't think that's on her agenda."

"I asked if it was on yours."

"I'm going to give my cousin a call," Josh said obliquely. "Pete—remember him? Mom's nephew. He's still in the phone book so he must have settled down here, and he's around my age. He could fix me up with a date or two, I'd imagine.''

"Hmmm...well, find out about Arabella first. You know, Josh, that's the best news I've had since I found out you were still alive,'' Graham finished buoyantly.

He sounded much younger than his sixty-two years. "I'll get back to you by Tuesday at the latest,'' Josh promised, and firmly changed the subject. "What's the weather like in Vancouver? They're issuing a snowfall warning here. Bit much for April."

They chatted for a few more minutes, then Josh hung up. He stared into the flames, hoping his father knew what he was doing. He, Josh, at fifteen had labeled Arabella as the scarlet woman who had broken up his parents' marriage; older now, and more cognizant of the essential coldness of his mother's nature, he nevertheless felt uneasy about Graham's insistence on reopening a relationship that had caused a great deal of pain to the six people who were most closely involved.

The book failed to hold his attention. After straightening the collar of his shirt under the cable-knit sweater he was wearing, and running a comb through his hair, he went downstairs.

Standing by the newel post, feeling rather foolish, he called, "Clem? Can I talk to you for a minute?"

From a door partway down the hall a muffled voice answered, "Just a sec," and was followed a moment later by Clem.

She was toweling her hair dry; it stood around her head in a bright aureole of tangled curls. She was wearing a forest green track suit under which she was definitely braless, and her feet were bare.

Josh said the second thing that came into his head. "How do you get a comb through that?"

"I've got a plastic pick." She chuckled. "The same kind of thing you'd use on a horse's mane and tail. I put the kettle on—want a cup of tea?"

"Sure," he said, abandoning his fire and his book without a second thought.

Her kitchen looked much as it might have a hundred years ago with its pine-board floor and antique pine table set by the window. The wallpaper had a design of entwined strawberries and tiny white blossoms; the curtains were lace. It was a friendly room, warm and cluttered and lived in. Clem sat down at the table, attacking her hair again with the towel. "The tea's out on the counter—choose whatever kind you like."

Her face was hidden. As her raised hands scrubbed at her scalp, her breasts moved under the loose folds of her sweater, whose waistband was rucked up to reveal a strip of pale, bare skin. His mouth suddenly dry, Josh dragged his eyes away and grabbed one of the packets on the counter. Red Zinger, the tea was called; it seemed appropriate.

Keeping his back to her, he found mugs and poured the boiling water into the teapot. Then he put everything on the table and sat down across from her. She had put the towel aside and was unscrewing the lid of a bottle of nail polish. Making his voice noncommittal with a manful effort, Josh asked, "Big date?"

"No... I rarely go out on Sundays. I bought this yesterday—do you think it's too bright?"

He smiled at her, storing away the information that Douglas, Jamie and the owner of the Mercedes were exiled from the house one day a week. "Have you ever seen an African tulip tree? It has big scarlet flowers much that color."

"Where does it grow?"

He described the savannah, then skirted away from the subject of Africa, telling her instead about the highlands in Papua New Guinea where he had lived in a camp for nearly two years. He poured himself a second mug of tea. Clem had painted her toenails and had started on her fingernails. Josh said, "I was talking to my father today and telling him about you—he's in Vancouver. He was wondering where your mother lives now."

The brush slipped and Clem got polish on her skin. "Damn!" she said. "Why would he want to know?"

"He wants to get in touch with her."

"I don't see the need for that."

"Is she living with someone—a man?"

"I told you she was on her own!"

His sea green eyes caught and held her stormy gray ones. "He'd like her address."

Her cheeks tinged with the same scarlet as her nails, Clem snapped, "I'd have to check with her first."

"She's a grown woman, Clem. If my father gets in touch with her and she doesn't want to see him, she can tell him so. It's not up to you to do that."

"Are you accusing me of meddling in my mother's life?"

"Yes," he said softly, "I believe I am."

"She's had enough problems with men. She doesn't need——"

Ruthlessly he interrupted. "She doesn't need you running interference for her."

"I'm not!" Jerkily she tried to screw the lid on the bottle.

"Yes, you are." Josh reached across the table and rested his hand over hers. "We don't have to fight over this, Clem—it's not our fight."

He could feel her anger and her confusion quivering through her fingertips. He held them in his own, smoothing them gently, and said, "Eighteen years ago we couldn't let our parents go, you and I. But now we have to."

She tugged her hand free; there were tears in her eyes. "You sure know how to get to me!" she choked. "I never cry, and here twice in a week I've felt like bawling my head off."

Josh said nothing, aware of compassion knifing his belly, a compassion Clem would undoubtedly reject. Arabella had had four different husbands; no wonder she was a loaded subject. Then Clem's mouth twisted in a self-deprecatory smile. "You're not saying anything, Joshua MacNeill, because you know whatever you say I'll bite your head off. Right?"

He wanted to put his arms around her and hold her; but he was sure she would resent that just as much as any facile words he might have come up with. "I like you, Clementina," he said spontaneously. "I like the way you're so honest with yourself."

Her eyes dropped. "I'll get my address book; I can never remember the postal code."

As she pushed back her chair Josh stood up too, walking around the table to stand close to her. Without touching her, because he was not quite sure he would be accountable if he did, he said, "Any time you want to bawl your head off, I've got a shoulder you can avail yourself of...okay?"

She tensed. "I've got certain rules as far as men are concerned. One of them is that I keep my troubles to myself."

A major part of his brain wondering what the rest of her rules were, Josh rejoined, "You're referring to the men you date. I'm different, Clem. I live here." He tweaked one of her curls. "You can let your hair down with me."

"I'm not so sure about that," she said breathlessly.

The pulse at the base of her throat was throbbing against her skin; he felt his blood thicken in response and forced himself to step back from her. "Think of me as your former stepbrother," he said.

"I'll get the address," she muttered, and fled the room.

Josh sat down hard in the nearest chair. He was going to call his cousin today, he thought grimly, and find a nice even-tempered brunette to date—he had always had a weakness for brunettes. Ms. Clementina Delaney with her mane of curls, her full breasts and her assorted hang-ups was not the woman for him.

He drained his mug, and when Clem came back copied Arabella's Toronto address on a piece of paper. "She's coming here for a visit in the next month," Clem said reluctantly.

"I'll look forward to seeing her again," Josh answered smoothly, getting up from the table again. "Thanks for the tea."

As soon as he was upstairs he telephoned Pete. His cousin was delighted to hear from him; they arranged to have lunch on Tuesday, and Pete invited him to a party he and his wife Mindy were giving the following Saturday. "Bring a friend," he said breezily. "It's pretty loose; Mindy and I are never quite sure who'll turn up at our parties."

"That's partly the reason I'm calling you," Josh said. "I'm out of touch in Halifax. The only female I know is my landlady."

"Are you saying you're unattached and available?"

"Yeah...Dad's even making noises about grand-children."

"Have I got prospects for you! Mindy's friend Sharon is coming to the party, our next door neighbor's divorced, one of my partners in the accountancy firm has moved out on her boyfriend—your phone'll be ringing off the hook. Don't attribute it all to your charm, though—there aren't many available men in this city.''

Clem seemed to manage fine, thought Josh. ''I'll look forward to Saturday night, then.''

''See you Tuesday, too. Glad you called, Josh.''

Josh put another log on the fire and went back to his book. There would be two phones in this house that would be ringing off the hook, he thought. One upstairs and one down.

Josh's book proved more engrossing than he had expected, and it was midnight before he put it down. When he went to draw the bedroom curtains he saw snow falling silently and purposefully from the sky, haloed by the street lights; it had been a long time since he had seen a real snowfall. Sparing a thought for the crocuses, he phoned his father with Arabella's address and went to bed.

He woke to wind, to the creaking of the house and to a rhythmic metallic scraping that he could not place. Swinging his legs to the floor, Josh drew back the curtain. In the cold gray light the snow whirled, ghostlike, above the roofs, spiraling over the chimneys, sheets of snow, ribbons of snow. The scraping was Clem, trying to shovel the gate clear of drifts that were thigh-deep.

It was seven-thirty in the morning.

He banged on the pane, trying to get her attention, but she was absorbed in her task. She was wasting her time. As fast as she shoveled the path clear the drifts reclaimed it, and why was she bothering anyway? She could not possibly go to work in this.

The bed, warm, rumpled, beckoned to him. Scowling, Josh pulled on his clothes and went downstairs, where he got his new waterproof jacket and rubber boots out of the cupboard. Pushing the front door open, he went out on the porch, where a second snow shovel was leaning against the wall. He picked it up and went down the steps.

For a moment, as if he were a little boy again, the scene delighted him. Snowflakes brushed his cheeks, and he opened his mouth, letting them melt on his tongue. Then Clem yelled, "Could you help me with the gate? Once that's clear I can leave."

He tramped down the path. "Leave? What for?"

Red-cheeked, droplets of melted snow clinging to her curls, she said, "To go to work, of course."

"You need a good strong cup of coffee," Josh said, taking her by the elbow. "I know it's a long time since I've lived in Halifax, but this qualifies as a Grade A Number One blizzard—nothing will be open today."

Leaning on her shovel, she glowered at him. "The daycare center will be open. We have mothers that have to work regardless of the weather, and one of the things we guarantee is that we never shut because of a storm. Christine lives out in Waverley and Louise in Sackville; they won't be able to get in. So it's up to me. Anyway, the radio said it was going to clear early this afternoon."

After this very comprehensive speech she went back to shoveling. "Are the buses running?" Josh asked.

"Late," she puffed. "I'm going to start off on foot."

"I've got a car—I'll drive you."

She looked up, her expressive features a mixture of hope, calculation and, undoubtedly, pleasure. "Would you, Josh? I'm worried about being late—I never thought it would take me this long to do the shoveling. The main road at the end of this street would be plowed ... and the street's downhill to there."

"Let's clean the car off," he said.

Twenty minutes later they were surging down the street, banners of snow flaring out from the wheels. Josh was enjoying himself; substitute a white stallion for his flashy red car and he was Sir Galahad in person, he thought immodestly. Then he saw the snowbank that the plow had left across the end of the street, a foot-high barrier between him and the main road. "Close your eyes," he said, and shifted gears.

Instead Clem tossed him a reckless grin. "How long did you say it was since you've driven in snow?"

"Ten years. But some things you never forget."

"I hope you're right."

The red car bucked its way through the snowbank and swung on to the road. Then it settled to a sedate pace up the hill. Clem patted the dashboard. "If I ever get the money I shall buy one of these," she vowed.

She was wearing a turquoise ski suit and the tip of her nose was red from the cold. Josh looked away, squinting through the ice-encrusted windshield. "Your parents had lots of money."

"They gave me the down payment for the house," she said. "First thing they'd cooperated on for years. But I won't take any more money from them. You see, Dad changed after the divorce—got out of the fast lane and bought a farm in Ontario. Ten years ago he married Marian, who's tiny and dumpy and the kindest person imaginable. She had three young children, so she and Dad don't have a whole lot of extra money, and I don't want them feeling responsible for me."

Marian sounded very different from Arabella. Fascinated, Josh asked, "And Arabella?"

"Alimony," Clem said briefly. "I won't touch it. Turn right at the next light."

There was ice under the snow at the intersections. Josh concentrated on staying in his lane and sincerely hoped he'd still be living in the house when Arabella came for a visit. Arabella and Clem in the same room was something he wanted to see.

There were three women with small children on the pavement outside the daycare center. The steps were heaped with snow. Josh parked on the side of the road and took the shovel from the back seat. "You open the place up," he said. "I'll shovel."

"Thanks," Clem said with a brilliant smile that no rescued princess could have bettered, and clambered over the bank to the waiting women.

Josh followed her, clearing off the steps first, then the pavement, then the driveway so he could park his car off the street. He was out of shape and there was a great deal of snow. When he had finished he clumped up the steps, knocked the snow from his boots and pushed the door open. It was not locked; Brad, just as well as he, could be going through the door.

The entrance hall was very warm. He struggled out of his jacket, left his boots on the tray and walked inside.

The heat hit him like a blow. The bright colors of the furniture and pictures suddenly wavered in his sight, blurring and running together; with horrible certainty he knew he had to sit down. The only chairs, little red wooden ones, had been made for three-year-olds. Josh slid his back along the wall and sat down hard on the floor, putting his head between his knees and praying Clem was otherwise occupied. Distantly he heard the harsh rhythm of his own breathing and felt sweat break out on his forehead. In London he had had these attacks regularly; but this was the first here.

A very small child of indeterminate sex waddled up to him and leaned heavily against his leg. "Peek-a-boo," it said.

As Josh looked up Clem came into the room. "Robin, I was—Josh!" she gasped.

She knelt beside him, putting a cool palm on his forehead and her other arm around his shoulders, her face so close to his that he could see each individual eyelash over the clear gray of her irises. "Josh, what's wrong? Are you ill?"

Her palm felt wonderful against his heated skin. Temporarily abnegating the role of Sir Galahad, he mumbled, "Out of shape."

"I keep forgetting you've been ill—you've looked so much better the last couple of days. You'd better go home and rest."

He had not been aware that she had been paying the least attention to the state of his health. He said more strongly, feeling laughter bubble in his chest, "I'm staying. To protect you."

She sat back on her heels. "What *are* you talking about?"

Robin, whose name had not settled the question of gender, climbed into Josh's lap and butted his chin. Josh added, "Is this a boy or a girl?"

"A boy, of course. Josh, are you delirious?"

His heart had stopped hammering in his ears and the red-painted fireplace was no longer slithering on to the green-painted hearth. He buried his face in Robin's belly, growled, "Peek-a-boo," and said, "You're all alone here except for a passel of kids, Clem, and I didn't like the look of your friend Brad. Give me ten minutes and I might even be able to keep him from coming in the door."

Robin gave a fat chortle, burrowed trustingly into Josh's shirtfront and began to suck his thumb. Josh, caught unawares by the child's solidity and warmth, instinctively put an arm around him and grinned down at him. "You're cute," he said.

"He's supposed to be having a rest."

"He can have it here. And I can guard the door at the same time."

"Brad has never once come in that door!"

"First time for everything." Abruptly Josh sobered. "I'm staying, Clem. And I'm driving you home this evening. What you do after that is your business."

In deference to Robin she kept her voice calm; but her eyes were blazing. "Do you remember the time you came to visit your father and my mother and me six months after the wedding? You ordered me around then just the same way."

He did remember that visit; it had been ghastly, with enough undercurrents to drown several stepchildren. "You've never buried the past, have you?" he said with brutal truth.

He watched fury flare in her face, and saw her fight to subdue it. She hissed, "I've got work to do. Just stay out of my way."

Robin stirred sleepily in Josh's arms. "Dad," he muttered, and closed his eyes.

The anger vanished from Clem's face, wiped from it like chalk from a blackboard. She reached over and tenderly ruffled Robin's hair. "He doesn't have a father," she murmured. "Never has had. He'll probably follow you around all day."

From the next room a child started to wail and there was the sound of tearing paper. "That'll be Michael," said Clem, rolling her eyes as she scrambled to her feet. Josh watched her go, and to his nostrils drifted the tantalizing scent of her perfume.

The day passed quickly. Josh played with Robin, read stories to two little girls called Emma and Marcie, was served soup and crackers for lunch by a polite but distant Clem, and shoveled more snow in the afternoon. Brad did not appear.

The other thing he did, as unobtrusively as he could, was watch Clem. She was very good with the children, firm, fair and loving; each child was obviously an individual to her and almost nothing escaped her notice. As much as was in her power she was giving these children stability, he decided, and thought again of Arabella's four marriages.

At five-twenty he backed his car out of the driveway, Clem beside him in the passenger seat, and headed for Weymouth Street. The sky was clear and the wind had died down. As the slush on the road grabbed at his tires, he said rhetorically, "Will summer ever come?"

"The snow doesn't last long at this time of year. I'll have to clean off some ground for the robins, though, poor things."

"You mean I get to shovel the garden too?" Josh teased.

"You've done enough for one day. Josh, I really am grateful for everything you did today...I don't know why I lose my temper with you so much."

"You mean you don't with Douglas, Jamie and the rest?"

"No...I suppose it's because you and I knew each other when we were younger. And not under the best of circumstances."

"Maybe you're right." Although he was not at all convinced that she was.

"I just hope you didn't do too much and wear yourself out."

The impressive physique of Jamie the football coach crossed his mind. He said irritably, "I'm thirty-three, not sixty."

"But you've been ill, you said so." They had stopped for a traffic light. Clem looked him full in the face and said, "You can tell me about it if you want to—the offer of a shoulder can go both ways, you know."

The light changed. The car behind Josh blew its horn. Josh swore under his breath and jerked his foot off the clutch. Clem added, "I thought a lot about what you said in the kitchen. You were quite right—we aren't dating, we're not involved, it's a bit like being brother and sister again. So we can confide in each other. Sort of a safety valve."

He didn't know which he disliked most: being thought of as a brother or as a safety valve. Why the devil hadn't he kept his mouth shut? He muttered something very rude as a taxi changed lanes in front of him and then remained conspicuously silent the rest of the way home. While Clem headed for the garden to replenish the bird feeders and talk to the robins, Josh went upstairs and ordered a pizza with the works for his supper; he was addicted to pizza and he didn't feel like cooking.

He could have ordered a medium pizza and shared it with Clem.

He ordered a small pizza instead.

CHAPTER THREE

By MIDEVENING Josh had calmed down. Flames were dancing cheerfully in the fireplace, a Schubert symphony was being broadcast on CBC stereo and he had a new Robert Ludlum to read. As the orchestra built to a crescendo he got up to put another log on the fire, stirring the other wood with the poker and absently watching the sparks shoot up the chimney. The brass and the percussion were giving it all they had; he had long ago decided that in his next incarnation he would like to be a trumpet player. Or perhaps a conductor...?

"Josh?"

His nerves, overstretched for too long in the prison, leaped; he dropped the poker with a clatter.

Clem was standing in the doorway. She said hastily, "Sorry—I didn't mean to startle you. I did call your name a couple of times."

Feeling rather foolish, for he had revealed something about himself he would have preferred to keep private, Josh turned the radio down. "Schubert must have drowned you out."

She was wearing jeans that fitted in all the right places, and a man's shirt; although her face and the shirt were streaked with dirt, her fingernails were still a vivid scarlet. He said formally, discovering he was very pleased to see her, "Will you sit down?"

She wrinkled her nose. "I can't. Do you know anything about furnaces?"

"The places I've lived, I know more about air conditioners. What's the trouble?"

"It won't go on. The repairman charges thirty-five dollars to come to the house before he even does anything, so if it's just something minor I'd rather not call him."

Josh carefully adjusted the screen in front of the fire. Thirty-five dollars did not seem like a lot of money to him, and she had the rent he was paying.

Perhaps his thoughts showed in his face. Clem said defensively, "I'm not tight with my money! But I had to put a new roof on the house last year, and I'm still paying for that."

Another small part of the puzzle that was Clem began to take shape in his mind. He said equably, "I don't think you're tight, Clem—you're a giver, not a taker. People who are tight have crimped-up little mouths." He then found himself staring at her mouth, which was soft and full and generous, and wondering what it would be like to kiss her...

She took a step backward. "You're a very exasperating man, do you know that? I never know what you're going to say next."

Josh dragged his mind away from a fantasy in which he was kissing her and discovering how perfectly she fitted into his arms; he disliked small, dainty women, they made him feel clumsy and loutish. "I have somewhat the same problem with you," he said. "Except you're a woman. Where's the furnace?"

She snorted, turned on her heel and led the way downstairs. Her hips moved beautifully in the faded jeans; she was indeed every inch a woman, thought Josh, and it was beginning to seem quite irrelevant that she wasn't a brunette.

The basement stairs led off the kitchen, narrow stairs hollowed by the passage of many feet. A small light bulb hung at the foot of the steps; the rest of the basement was in darkness. Josh felt his nerves tighten. The ceiling was low enough that he had to stoop, the floor was dirt and one entire wall was a huge slab of granite on which part of the house was resting. He took a couple of deep breaths. It was only a basement. He was in Halifax, with Clem. Not in Africa. He was safe.

Clem, her head bent, had crossed the floor and was edging her way past a stack of old storm windows. "The furnace is back here," she said. "There's a bulb burned out—I should have brought a flashlight."

Crouched low, Josh made it past the windows. His palms were sweating, and the pressure building in his brain. Every nerve in his body screamed at him to run; he stumbled on a protruding rock and heard Clem say, "Behind here—can you see?"

In front of him was a passageway, a black rectangle leading into darkness. Josh stopped in his tracks, as if he had slammed into a cement wall, and said in a voice so thin that it didn't sound like his, "I can't go in there."

Clem peered back at him. "What did you say?"

He grabbed at the wall for support, his fingers wrapping themselves around the slate rocks of the foundation, his knuckles white. His face was probably the same dead white; he was making a fool of himself. "I can't go in there," he repeated numbly. "I've got claustrophobia."

Another regrettable side effect, the London doctors had told him. It would pass in time. Nothing to worry about.

Clem was standing right in front of him without his having any very clear idea of how she had got there. She touched his arm, which was rigid from shoulder to wrist. "You should have told me."

He was suddenly tired of all he was hiding from her. He drew a ragged breath and said as succinctly as he could, "I spent the last two years in Africa—one of those new republics near the coast—doing some legal work on mining contracts for the oil company I worked for. There's been a civil war going on there for years. I got careless, I saw more than I should have, and they threw me in prison. Five months of solitary confinement in an underground room...that's where I got ill, and that's why I can't stand small spaces, especially if they're dark."

He seemed to have run out of words. Clem said strongly, "Come on upstairs. I'll pour you a stiff drink of rum and I'll call the furnace man." With firm fingers she detached his hand from the wall and, taking him by the wrist, led him toward the stairs. Her fingers felt very warm on his cold skin.

The kitchen was brightly lit. Josh said bitterly, "I nearly pass out after shoveling a bit of snow and I can't go near the furnace because I'm afraid of the dark— you want to change tenants? You'd be better off with a woman."

Clem plunked a bottle of rum on the counter so hard that the liquid sloshed up to the cap. "Josh, you're far too intelligent and sophisticated a man to go the macho, if-I'm-physically-less-than-a-hunk-I'm-no-good-as-a-man route. No, I don't want to change tenants. Coke or water?"

He felt a glow of pleasure that she didn't want to be rid of him; the black hole in the basement retreated a little. "Coke. Please," he said. "Hey, take it easy on the rum; you'll be carrying me up to bed."

"I'd be leaving you to sleep it off on the kitchen floor," she amended glibly, passing him the glass. She then made her phone call and said in a resigned voice, "He'll be here in twenty minutes."

The rum slid down Josh's throat. She was generous with her drinks, too, he thought, and said, "Why do you keep the house when you have to worry about every penny?''

She sat down across from him at the pine table. "Because I love it." The cool gray eyes dared him to challenge her.

He decided to push his luck. "An old house that needs thousands of dollars spent on it and a garden that's too big for you. That's not love, that's masochism."

"I've just discovered something," Clem said dulcetly. "One reason I keep losing my temper with you is because you're so rude."

"Go ahead, Clem," he said lazily, "lose it now—you know you're dying to. After a whole week of being nice to Douglas and Jamie and that stodgy-looking guy with the Mercedes, you're due to let your hair down."

"That stodgy-looking guy, whose name is Duncan Copley, happens to be one of the most respected lawyers in the city——"

"Dull as ditchwater," said Josh, and watched outrage and amusement battle in her eyes.

"His opinions are a touch conservative," she admitted. "But he's on the board of the symphony and that has to count for something."

Josh leaned forward. "But does Handel touch his soul?"

"You really know where to put the knife, don't you?" she remarked. "Do you have a problem with my dating different men, Josh? Because there are several you haven't met yet."

He had been afraid of that. "And what if you decided to marry one of them? You'd have to sell the house."

She took a gulp of her drink and said with considerable emphasis, "I don't want to get married. Nor will I ever sell the house."

"Why not?"

"You really want to know?" she asked, her eyes glittering. "Okay! The abbreviated version of Clementina Linton-MacNeill-Fougere-Delaney's life. To start with, my father was in the armed forces. That house on Young Avenue where we lived across the street from you was the fifth house I'd lived in by the age of ten. When my mother married your father we moved to Ontario. They divorced; another move. Mom married Andrew Fougere. We lived on his ranch in Alberta for three years. They divorced. We moved back to Toronto. She married Eric Delaney and we moved into his town house. They divorced. I left home and went to university, first up there and then here in Halifax. I lived in residence and then in an apartment, and then this house went on the market and I asked my parents for money—the only time in my life I have and the only time I will. This house is *mine*. I can stay in it forever if I want to, and never have to move again."

Josh said mildly, "That makes perfect sense."

Her nostrils flared. "You're not going to argue with me?"

"No." Or touch you or offer you sympathy, he thought. Because you'd probably belt me if I did.

"Oh." She looked mollified and deflated at the same time. "The house is nearly two hundred years old; it was on a big estate once. Now all that's left of the land is the double lot. There's a real estate agent wants to buy half the garden from me to build a fancy cedar home on it, but I won't sell."

Josh's drink was nearly gone and the furnace man would be arriving soon. "I would presume Arabella's four divorces are the reason you don't want to marry?"

"Well, of course." Clem's mouth curved in a smile full of self-mockery. "You don't have to be a psychologist to figure that one out, do you? Mentioning marriage and permanence in the same breath to me is like putting catsup on crêpes Suzette. They just don't go together.''

Josh drained his glass, put it carefully on the table and said, ''In some ways we're alike, Clem. I haven't lived in anything resembling a civilized place for the last ten years, and I'm tired of that—I came to Halifax to settle down, put down some roots.'' He gave her a thoughtful look. ''And that's where we part company. Because settling down for me includes marriage. A lasting commitment. Children. The whole deal.''

''And who do you have in mind for the post of wife and mother?'' she asked in a brittle voice.

''No one yet. I've only been here ten days.''

The doorbell chimed. Clem got up with evident relief, said ironically, ''She'll be a most fortunate woman,'' and swept out of the room as well as anyone could who was wearing jeans and an oversize shirt.

Josh rinsed out his glass, was introduced to the furnace man and went up to bed.

On Tuesday Josh had lunch with his cousin Pete, whose hairline had receded and whose sense of humor had become a little less raunchy in the intervening years, and who had added a wife and baby to his life. Josh admired the photos of a pretty blonde holding a plump but otherwise undistinguished infant, and gave a condensed version of his own adventures since he had left Halifax. Pete then extolled the virtues of Sharon, among which was the fact that she was a brunette. He also suggested Josh meet him after work on Thursday for a drink. ''I'll bring my partner along, the one whose boyfriend moved out. You should play the field, Josh.'' He nodded sagaciously. ''It would be a mistake to marry the first woman you meet.''

"My landlady?" said Josh. "No way."

Said landlady went out with the football coach on Tuesday evening and introduced Josh to an extremely handsome man named Manuel on Wednesday. So it gave Josh considerable pleasure to feel he had a date on Thursday. Pete's partner Judy was a sleek, sophisticated blonde, who was both bright and ambitious; she flirted expertly, had a cutting sense of humor and would be more than the equal of any man who tried to stand in her way. Josh admired her drive, laughed rather wryly at some of her jokes, and found himself contrasting Judy's gloss with Clem's tangled curls and far less calculated emotions. He did not suggest another date; he could not picture himself married to Judy.

When he got home about ten, Douglas's battered little car was parked outside the house and the doors to Clem's living room and bedroom were both closed. Josh made as much noise as he could going up the stairs, and flipped on the television for the national news, turning the volume up high.

The news was followed by a program assessing the political status of various African nations, which involved a short clip on the rebellion in which he had inadvertently been caught up. He forced himself to watch it, and sat doggedly until the program was over before going to bed.

Douglas's car had gone. Josh climbed into the brass bed, drawing the covers over his bare shoulders as the house creaked and sighed like an old lady settling for the night. He hoped Sharon, whom he was to meet on Saturday, was less sharp-edged than Judy. Comparing Judy to Clem, for instance, was like comparing an extra dry martini to a full-bodied burgundy. Not that Clem was in any way his standard for a mate...

*   *   *

The dream always followed the same pattern. A jungle clearing, the only sound the discordant screeching of a parrot. The sense of being watched, of a gathering menace. His headlong flight through the forest, leaves as big as dinner plates slapping his face, vines tripping him, leeches clinging to his skin; and the enemy ever closer, unseen, infinitely frightening. His legs getting heavier and heavier, slower and slower to move. Then the fall into a black hole which closed over his head, enveloping him in darkness so thick as to be tangible. The first tentative movements of his feet and his horror-stricken discovery that on the floor of beaten earth were scattered the bodies of his friends, who had died here, forgotten. As he would be forgotten. As he would die. And then the dream's climax, when he went berserk, pounding the low roof with his fists, yelling at the top of his voice, yelling, screaming, and the sound swallowed by the darkness as if it had never been...

Someone was shaking him, crying his name. "Wake up, Josh! Josh, wake *up*."

He tore his arm free and struck out—because who could it be but one of the soldiers?—and felt against the back of his hand a woman's softness.

"Stop it—it's me, Clem!"

Still in the grip of the nightmare, Josh hauled himself up in the bed, shaking his head to try and clear it. His chest heaving, his breathing raw in his throat, he gasped, "Clem? Is that you?"

The only light in the room came from the street lamp outside; in its amber glow he saw the dark outline of a woman. She leaned toward him, clasping him by the shoulders. "Oh, Josh, are you all right? You frightened me..."

"God, Clem, I'm sorry——"

"It's okay. Just as long as you're awake."

As his vision adjusted to the light, he could see her eyes, huge, almost black. Black as the hole in which he had been trapped. The images of the dream swirled around him, the terror heavy as lead in his chest. In a simple need for comfort, for the warmth of another human being, he pulled her toward him and buried his face in her hair. His mother had been neither a maternal nor an emotional woman; there had been very little in the way of motherly softness when he had been a boy.

As reality gradually usurped the dream, Josh realized the woman in his arms was very lightly trembling. Clem was not a woman to scare easily. "Clem, I'm sorry," he repeated, and unconsciously tightened his arms around her.

With a jolt in his belly he became aware of other sensations. The heat of her palms on his back; from years of being in the tropics, he always slept naked. The fragrance of her hair and the softness of her breasts against his chest. With another jolt he remembered how his fist had struck that softness. He raised his head, searching out the blackness of her eyes. "I hit you—I didn't mean to."

"You pack a wallop," she said with a shaky grin. "Remind me never to seriously annoy you... I came upstairs because you were yelling. You woke me up... I— I thought you were being murdered."

"A nightmare," he said dryly.

"Perfect example of a redundant statement," said Clem with a slightly more convincing grin, drawing back a little from his embrace. "You really scared me."

Her hair was loose, a cloud of curls around her face. She was wearing a long housecoat, dull blue in the gloom, that she had hastily belted around her waist; it gaped at the neck, exposing the swell of her breasts and the shadow of her cleavage. He remembered the soft, yielding flesh that he had struck, and briefly closed his eyes, trying to pull her closer again. But she resisted him, her fingers tangled in the dark hair on his chest as she pushed against him. "Tell me about the dream—what it's like," she said. "Why you were shouting so horribly."

She eased free of him, tucking her feet under her and wrapping them in the folds of the housecoat, her body a graceful curve against the pallor of the wallpaper. Part of him wanted to tell her about the dream, for maybe in the telling it would lose some of its hold on him; but another part wanted nothing of words. This part told Josh to draw her close again and kiss her, kiss her until she trembled from something other than fear; and then to explore the slender, vibrant body that he had all too briefly held in his arms.

He clamped down on his own thoughts. Seducing Clem, even in fantasy, was no part of his plan to settle down and get married. Even if she would have him, which he doubted. He twisted in the bed, thumping on the pillows as he rearranged them behind his head, then hauling the covers partway up his chest. Not giving himself time to think, because if he did he'd probably clam up, he said, "In the basement I only told you part of the story... I'd been living in a compound on the outskirts of the capital city, but I spent quite a lot of time out in the bush and got very friendly with the young couple who were helping to run a missionary hospital— they were both doctors. Caroline and Hans." He gave a reminiscent chuckle. "She was a demon poker player, and Hans loved to play the flute...we had some great evenings."

"Were they American?"

"She was Australian and he was Dutch." Wanting to get this over with, he went on, "I had to go to London for a conference, and when I got back there were rumors that there'd been trouble in the village nearest the hospital. I went up there right away in a borrowed jeep." His voice hardened. "The village had been burned to the ground and the hospital was badly damaged. No one knew what had happened to Caroline and Hans...I found them the next day. They'd been—shot. I was loading the bodies in the jeep when the rebels came back. I suppose I was damn lucky they didn't shoot me, just threw me in jail instead."

"For five *months*? Didn't anyone come looking for you?"

"The rebels were using me as a lever at the bargaining table—I found that out afterward." His smile was wry. "It would have been nice to have known it at the time. Instead I just thought they'd forgotten me."

"It must have been awful," Clem said in a low voice. "No wonder you have nightmares."

He plucked at the edge of the sheet, the semidarkness giving him the courage to fill in the details: the mock execution the soldiers had staged, out of boredom, with himself as victim; the times they had forgotten to feed him; the crushing sense of abandonment and loneliness. Then he looked up. "I've never talked about it this much to anyone. They had a high-powered shrink from Harley Street come to see me in the hospital, but it was all too new then and I more or less sent him packing."

Clem managed a small laugh. "I can picture the scene."

"My language was not propitiatory."

"An unresolved Oedipal complex, no doubt." She was peering at him through her lashes, with a sly grin. He was suddenly aware of the old house slumbering around them, and of this woman, whom he had known as a gawky young girl, who was now perched on his bed in the middle of the night. A very beautiful woman with an enticing valley between her breasts and a mass of untidy, sweet-scented hair. His mouth dry, he wondered what it would be like to have her lying beside him sharing his pillow, to loosen the belt of her housecoat and let his hand drift beneath it...

"Well," said Clem, sitting up straight and tightening the belt of her housecoat, "it must be late, I'd better get back to bed."

She sounded flustered. Josh said truthfully, "I'm wide-awake."

She favored him with another of those endearing grins. "So am I, actually. How about hot chocolate and cookies in the kitchen?" She reached out a hand. "Come on."

He let her pull him partway up, then said casually, "I haven't got anything on, Clem."

She dropped his hand as if it were scalding her and in an interesting flurry of bare legs stood up by the bed. "I'll go and put the milk on," she said in a strangled voice, and was out of the door before he could reply.

Josh also stood up, picking up his jeans from the chair and pulling them on. Clem was twenty-eight years old and by no means uninterested in men; yet she had just acted as shyly as any virgin. The more he saw of her, the more of a mystery she became. And, he had to admit, the more intriguing she became, too. He put on a long-sleeved shirt, left the buttons undone, and went downstairs.

The overhead light shone brightly on the table; no more confidences in the half light, thought Josh, and opened the cookie tin which was sitting on the counter. "Mmm," he said, "chocolate chip—my favorite kind." He took a large one and bit into it, then said with his mouth full, "Beats me how you've managed to discourage all your men friends from marriage...your cookies alone are worth a trip to the altar."

She was standing by the stove stirring the saucepan; flashing him a bright smile, she said, "It's easy. I just say no."

"So tell me about them. But you can leave out the lawyer, I didn't like his looks."

She reached up in the cupboard for two mugs, her housecoat pulled tight across her breasts; Josh took another cookie. "I met Jamie, the football coach, last year when his little boy was in the daycare center," she said obediently. "Jamie's a widower and he's in no hurry to remarry, he really loved his wife and I think he's afraid to fall in love again. So with him I'm safe, you see. Manuel's a man-about-town with no desire whatsoever to settle down. As for Douglas, he's a fourth-year medical student who's dirt poor and doesn't get enough to eat and wants to be a surgeon—so he certainly can't get married to an impecunious daycare worker." She poured the hot chocolate into the mugs and added generous handfuls of marshmallows. "So that takes care of three of them."

"Brad?"

"Brad was not one of my smarter moves. I met him in a bar, he had tickets to a rock concert I wanted to go to—my tastes aren't always as elevated as Handel—and so off we went. Then he decided he wanted to go to bed with me, and when I declined—rather gracefully, I thought—he got a bit nasty. Not used to having women say no, I would suspect—he's a very good-looking guy in a kind of a sinister way. So no more dates with Brad."

"Do you always decline gracefully, Clem?"

"Sometimes not so gracefully."

"And sometimes not at all?"

She poked at a marshmallow floating near the top of her mug. Although her cheeks were a little pinker than the heat of the drink warranted, she met his gaze levelly.

"Do you really think that's any of your business?" she asked.

"You sure got out of my room in a hurry."

"That was because you looked as though you were mentally undressing me," she answered hotly.

"A temporary aberration. I'm sorry," Josh said, and wondered if either part of that statement was true. He was basically an honest man; maybe it was time he met Sharon. "You didn't answer the question," he added.

"I don't intend to."

Liking her stubbornness, he said, "So tell me about the other men."

"Stewart is a sports fan who takes me to hockey games in the winter and baseball games in the summer, and Paul dates me when he gets depressed because the woman he loves won't marry him." She bit into a cookie. "Those are the main ones."

"Not a bad total for a city that according to my cousin has a few available men."

"It's my girlish charm," she said limpidly.

"It's your chocolate chip cookies."

As she raised her mug to her lips, she kept her eyes fastened on his. "If there's a lack of men, you shouldn't have any problem finding yourself a woman."

"Why do I feel as though I've been not so subtly insulted?" Josh asked, getting up and rinsing his empty mug in the sink. "The campaign starts tomorrow."

Anger flared in her eyes. "You sound so cold-blooded about an issue that's emotional."

He was angry himself, although he couldn't quite put his finger on the reason. "Clem, you go out with different men because there's safety in numbers. I'm planning to go out with different women because I want to be sure when I marry that it'll last. I know neither of my parents married four times like Arabella—but I didn't like the divorce either, and I sure as heck don't want one of my own."

"I'm sorry," she said stiffly, "I shouldn't have said that."

She looked so chastened that his anger melted as quickly as it had risen. "It's okay, I lost my cool."

She got up and rinsed out her own mug; Josh was standing between her and the door. "Well, good night," she said lamely.

As she walked past him, he grasped her hand and said, "Clem, thanks for waking me up. And thanks for listening, too." Then, driven by an impulse he had been repressing for several days, he leaned over and kissed her full on the mouth.

He felt a tiny shock of surprise ripple through her, then the instinctive yielding of her lips beneath his. Her breath was sweet, her skin smooth as silk; he brought his free hand up to her face, stroking her hair back, delighting in the flowing curve from cheekbone to ear. Fighting to keep his kiss gentle, undemanding, because the tension was building in her body, he felt his heart begin to beat in thick, heavy strokes; and knew there were demands he wanted to make.

Then she tugged her hand free and pushed against his chest with both palms. "Josh, don't!" she choked.

"Why not?" he said breathlessly. "We're not children, Clem."

"Because you'll spoil everything," she said fiercely.

There were hectic patches of color in her cheeks, and her eyes were turbulent. I want to make love to her, Josh thought dazedly. I want to carry her up to my bed and strip off her housecoat and imprint my body on every inch of hers.

Which was definitely not part of his strategy to settle down and find a wife.

As if she had read his thoughts, Clem seethed, "You're looking for a wife—you said so. But I don't want to be anyone's wife. So we're certainly not going to get sexually involved just because we live in the same house." She glared up at him. "How long since you've been with a woman, Josh?"

"Too long, obviously," he snapped, wanting to shake her, wanting to kiss her again, wanting to touch her breasts so badly that he ached with the need, then hating himself—and her—for this need.

She looked, if anything, relieved by his response. "It's not really me, then," she said. "Anyone would do."

He was damned if she was going to get away with that. "Don't be naive!"

"You're ruining it," she retorted. "How can we have hot chocolate at three in the morning if you're going to put the make on me?"

"Now you're being crude! I only kissed you because I was grateful."

"Ha! It might have started that way——"

He said flatly, "You liked it too, Clem."

Her eyes fell. "I'm going to bed," she said, and stalked out of the room.

Josh put the lid back on the cookie tin, switched out the light and climbed the stairs to his own bed. It seemed distressingly wide and very empty. When he did finally go to sleep, he dreamed again, a highly erotic dream with Clem as its protagonist. He woke with an erection and with the resolve never to kiss her again.

As part of his resolve he went downtown on Saturday morning and bought himself jogging shoes, a sweat suit and rain gear. It was time he started getting back in shape; and exercise would sublimate his sexual energy and keep him out of trouble with Clem or anyone else. He hoped.

That afternoon he did two miles, walking and running, and was discouraged by how tired he felt when he got back to the house. After he had a shower and washed his hair, he lay down on the bed for five minutes, and woke up at eight-thirty. The party at Pete's started at eight-thirty. Not in the mood to hurry, Josh made supper, washed the dishes and put on dress pants, a new shirt and a heavy-knit sweater he had bought on Saturday as well, its mingling of blues and greens deepening the color of his eyes.

As he pulled it over his head, he heard the front door bang. Clem, going out. He scowled at himself in the mirror, wondering who she was with tonight. Darned if he was going to look.

Smoothing down his hair, he decided he looked better than he had ten days ago, his face filling out and losing that sallow hue, his step with more spring in it. He picked up his car keys and headed down the steps, whistling jauntily. It would be nice if Sharon bowled him off his feet. It would take his mind off his harridan of a landlady with her numerous men friends and her big gray eyes . . .

CHAPTER FOUR

PETE and Mindy lived in a new three-level town house near one of the universities; the party appeared to be flourishing on all three levels by the time Josh arrived. Pete pulled him in the door. "I was beginning to think you'd forgotten," he yelled above the noise. "No more room in the closet there—take your coat up to the master bedroom, Josh, and then come on down and meet Mindy and I'll get you a drink. Sharon hasn't arrived yet; she said she'd be a little late."

Josh climbed the two sets of stairs, his calf muscles protesting. There were three bedrooms on the third floor, but only one with lights on. He took off his trenchcoat and walked in.

Clem was standing in front of the mirror applying her lipstick.

He saw her a couple of seconds before she saw him, long enough for him to be aware of surprise, a natural enough reaction, and of an intense pleasure, a reaction that irritated him out of all proportion. He flung his coat on the bed. "Hello, Clem."

The hand holding the lipstick jerked; a smear of red gashed the corner of her mouth. Ignoring it, she said rudely, "What are *you* doing here?"

"Pete's my cousin. I could ask the same of you."

"Jamie is Mindy's brother."

He stared at her reflection in the mirror. She looked magnificent. Her hair was loose around her face in a great mane, inevitably reminding him of the night she had sat on his bed and listened to his story; her makeup was dramatic; and her jumpsuit, kingfisher blue, tightly sashed, outlined the curves of her figure in a way calculated to inspire lust in any man under eighty. Her earrings, big gold parrots, were gently bumping against the creamy skin of her throat.

He said huskily, "You belong in a tropical forest under a tulip tree ... color and heat and the prowl of the lion."

His reflection loomed behind hers in the mirror, the blue of his eyes the blue of the fabric that clung to her body at breast and hip. He could see her struggling to reduce his words to the banality of a compliment, and failing utterly. Nor could she drag her eyes from his. Her breast rose and fell; when she bit her lip and thereby transferred some of the lipstick to her teeth, he felt his heart melt with what could only be called tenderness.

Someone walked in the bedroom door.

Clem jerked her gaze to the newcomer and said with transparent relief, "Hello ... it's Sharon, isn't it?"

Josh winced. And winced again when he saw that Clem had noticed his reaction. Swift comprehension flashed across her face. With the merest breath of malice she said, "Josh, you haven't yet met Sharon, have you? Sharon Lindquist—I've got it right, haven't I, Sharon? We've met once or twice at the swimming pool, remember? Sharon, this is Josh MacNeill."

Sharon's lashes flickered at the mention of his name; Clem undoubtedly noticed that too, thought Josh, aware of a reprehensible urge to burst out laughing. Then, with an aplomb that made him want to shake her, Clem plucked a Kleenex from the flowered box on the dresser and started to repair her lipstick.

Josh's mother might not have been a demonstrative woman, but she had instilled good manners in her only child. Josh shook Sharon's hand and said, "Nice to meet you, Sharon—Pete's told me about you. Here, let me help you with your coat."

After lifting the pretty yellow wool coat from her shoulders and laying it on the bed, he said, glancing over at Clem in the mirror, "Shall we go down and find the bar?"

"You go ahead," Clem said lightly. "I'll be down in a minute."

Sharon left the room ahead of him. So he could not look back at Clem, Josh took a quick inventory of Sharon's appearance. She was wearing a pale yellow angora sweater with dark brown leather pants; she was slim, much shorter than Clem, her cap of brunette hair shining under the lights. When she stopped on the landing to wait for him, he added dark, lively eyes and a vivacious, heart-shaped face. As they started down the stairs together, she said forthrightly, "You know Clem?"

"I'm renting the top floor of her house. I moved in two weeks ago."

"She's a very fine person—she's done a lot for daycare centers in the city. But you probably know that."

"No...I grew up in Halifax but I've been away for years, so I've lost touch with the political scene."

"She's lobbied for years for more daycare centers, especially for lower income parents, and for pay increases for the daycare workers—their salary levels are disgracefully low. And on top of that, of course, she loves children. That's a rarer attribute than you might think in the ranks of those that deal with children." Sharon wrinkled her charming, uptilted nose. "Just ask me. I'm a teacher—I know. So for Clem to combine a gutsy political attitude with genuine caring for the kids she looks after is quite amazing...thank goodness for the Clems of this world."

Josh stored this information away and said, rather heavy-handedly because he didn't want to talk about Clem, "Where do you teach, Sharon?"

She was quite intelligent enough to assess his change of subject; but she went along with it. "Park Street High."

"When I was growing up, that was the toughest school in town."

"Still is," she said cheerfully. "I teach grade ten French. I work for three years on deferred salary, then take every fourth year off and travel—that way I keep my sanity."

As they eased their way to the bar, they found out they had both been in Turkey at the same time two years ago. Sharon was a good conversationalist, and as they mingled with other friends of hers, and danced in the rec room, and helped themselves from the buffet in the dining room, Josh knew he liked her and would be happy to spend more time with her. Which did not stop him from keeping what he hoped was an unobtrusive eye on Clem.

She looked as if she was having a marvelous time. As did Jamie, who was surely what any female with hormones would call a hunk. And what better a female companion could he have than a woman who would love his little boy and put no pressure on him to recover from the loss of his first wife?

As the dancing speeded up, Jamie whirled Clem in a circle and she collapsed, laughing, in his arms. There was an ease between them, thought Josh painfully: the ease of sexual partners who were comfortable with each other?

Sharon said softly, "You don't look very happy."

Josh's eyes flew back to her face. "Sorry," he said with a gaucheness unusual to him.

"You're very attracted to Clem, aren't you?"

He and Sharon had been dancing in one corner of the room and were isolated both by the music and by the motion of the other couples on the floor, none of whom was paying them the slightest attention. Josh grimaced. "No! Of course not," he said, and wondered whom he was trying to convince.

"She's a very beautiful woman."

Her face looked pinched and unhappy. Chiding himself for his insensitivity, Josh began, "Sharon, I——"

She put a hand on his wrist. "Josh, we both know Pete's setting us up, we knew that before we came tonight. Please don't get me wrong—I like you very much. The trouble is, I've been in love with Jamie for months."

It was an ironic twist to the plot that Josh would never have thought of. In a rush of admiration for her honesty and courage, he put his arms around her, smiling down at her with real warmth. "I like you, too," he said. "Why don't we get out of here and go somewhere quieter where we can talk? The bar at Harbour's Edge is very pleasant."

"I'd like that," Sharon said, and smiled back.

She was a lovely young woman, and his blood was quite unmoved. Then, warned by a prickling on the back of his neck, he looked around. Clem was watching them, her body in the blue jumpsuit absolutely still, her face a mask he was quite unable to interpret. When she realized he had seen her, she tossed her head, as proud as any lion, wrapped her arms around Jamie's neck and began to dance with him rather more closely than was discreet. Josh looked back at Sharon. "Hell," he said succinctly.

"At least," she responded, her dark eyes full of pain.

"Let's find Pete and Mindy and get out of here."

"Pete'll put the worst possible interpretation on our leaving early, you realize that?"

"You get our coats. I'll look after Pete."

Sharon raised her brows. "No need to look quite so aggressive. I'll be down in a minute."

Half an hour later they were sitting across from each other in a piano bar, in velvet-covered chairs by a tall window overlooking the harbor. Josh raised his drink. "Better days ahead, Sharon. Tell me how you met Jamie."

"We quite literally bumped into each other in the supermarket three months after his wife died—we knocked down a pile of cereal boxes. When we tried to pick them up, he touched me by accident and the whole world shifted . . . just as the poets say it should. It did for him, too—that's the awful part. We went out on a couple of dates, we ended up in bed on the third one, and right afterward Jamie decided we shouldn't see each other again. It was too soon for him and he didn't want to get involved. Shortly after that I met him out with Clem, and they've been dating off and on ever since." She took a handful of peanuts from the bowl on the table. "End of story. Now it's your turn."

Josh explained the saga of his and Clem's parents, and described how he had more or less manipulated Clem into renting the apartment to him. "We've never had a date together—how could we, she's too busy dating half the rest of Halifax?—and I've only kissed her once. She's driving me up the wall."

"*My* only comfort is that according to all her friends she swears she'll never get married."

"That's the message I get loud and clear."

"She and Jamie'll probably still be dating when he's fifty," Sharon said darkly.

"How long is it now since his wife died?"

"A year and two months."

"Why don't you phone him up and suggest you go for a walk together, something casual that wouldn't put any pressure on him?"

"Two reasons. One, he might say no. Two, he might say yes and I'll discover that for him the world no longer shifts—I'm just an embarrassing memory. Someone he'd rather forget. He didn't make any opportunity to speak to me tonight, for instance." Her slim fingers toyed restlessly with her glass. "I don't think Clem, to do her justice, has any idea there was ever anything between Jamie and me. He wouldn't be likely to tell her."

Josh wanted to believe this because he didn't like to think of Clem cheating in any way. "Finish your drink and we'll go find a dance floor in one of the bars," he said, wanting to lift the misery from Sharon's face; she was a lively and enthusiastic dancer. "And then next weekend, if you're free, we'll have dinner together and go to a movie."

"Actually, I'm going home for the weekend, my parents live in the Annapolis Valley. But I have two tickets for the Royal Winnipeg Ballet on Thursday... they're performing Thursday, Friday and Saturday. Would you like to go with me?"

"Love to," Josh said promptly. "I'll take you to dinner first. Dress up—we'll go somewhere fancy."

"You're a nice man, Joshua MacNeill," Sharon said. "Let's go dance!"

And dance they did, until two in the morning. Josh then delivered Sharon to the lobby of her apartment building, and drove home. As he flicked on the turn signal for Clem's driveway a blue car he recognized as Jamie's was just pulling away from the curb. So Clem was home.

How long had she been home? Had she and Jamie gone to bed together?

He strode up the path and took the front steps two at a time. His key stuck in the lock. Swearing at it, he jerked the door open. Clem was standing in the hall pulling off her boots.

So she and Jamie had not been to bed together. He gave her a wide grin and said ebulliently, "Did you have a good time tonight?"

She kicked off her second boot and said in a clipped voice, "Thank you, yes. Good night." Whipping the scarf from around her neck, she fired it at the coat stand; she missed, and the scarf fluttered to the floor. She and Josh reached for it at the same time and their hands brushed.

As clearly as if Sharon were standing there, her voice replayed in Josh's mind..."we touched and the earth moved...just as the poets say it should." As Clem grabbed the scarf, he took her by the wrist, pinning it to the floor; from sheer surprise her wrist went limp, and beneath his index finger he felt the steady throbbing of her pulse, the very voice of her blood. This astounding and unexpected intimacy shot right through his body; his own pulse quickened and everything in the world dropped away but for the wide-spaced gray eyes only inches away and the whisper of her breathing.

Then, beneath his fingertips, her pulse began to race.

Once, in the desert, Josh had held a dove that a falcon had wounded; its pulse had raced in his hand in the same way, and in the yellow eyes fear and a rage for life had mingled in a way that had struck him to the heart.

Clem was afraid; he knew it in his bones. And even as he watched, she took refuge in anger. The tendons in her wrist tensed. She said evenly, "Josh, let go."

His answer was to pull her to her feet, and with an arm around her waist draw the length of her body against his, so that they touched at knee and hip and breast. Then he stood still and waited.

For him time stopped. Her body fitted so perfectly into his that his arousal was instant and primitive and fierce; her face changed as he moved against her. He bent his head and began kissing her.

He was drowning, drowning in the pliant promise of her body and the tentative but unmistakable response of her lips. He let go of her wrist and wound his arms around her, deepening his kiss and achingly aware of the generosity with which she opened to him. As his tongue danced between her lips, the shock rippled through her. He murmured her name, gentling his demands, trying to attune himself to her, to give rather than take, and felt her arms wind themselves around his neck and the fullness of her breasts shift against his chest. He kissed her again, exulting in the ardor with which she responded, an ardour that was somehow touchingly shy.

He left her mouth, tracing the curve of her cheek, the closed lids, the sweep of her forehead, wanting to capture the essence of her through his lips, then burying his face in the soft tangle of her hair. "Your hair smells of pine trees," he muttered. "I want you more than I've ever wanted a woman before."

To him this was a simple and self-evident truth; he wasn't prepared for the sudden rigidity of Clem's body, nor for the strength with which she twisted free of his embrace. She looked aghast, as though she had lost her bearings, and her voice was shaking as she whispered, "Why are we doing this? I must be out of my mind!"

Her eyes were wild, her face full of terror. Josh remembered the dove, said forcefully, "There's nothing to be afraid of, Clem," and realized he was speaking to himself as much as to her. For a moment ago he had spoken the truth: Clem, in one kiss, had reached a part of him that had never been touched before. He had had affairs in the ten years that he had wandered the globe, but no woman had ever surged through him as Clem had, like a wave of the sea.

She was clutching her scalp with both hands in a gesture of unconscious drama, her hair in more than its usual disarray. "That mustn't happen again," she said. "There's no place in my life for you, Josh—I mean that. I'm not being coy, I'm not playing games. I just don't want to get involved." Then she tilted her chin in a way he was beginning to realize was characteristic of her and added sharply, "Anyway, you spent the evening with Sharon, and you sure left the party in a hurry. Did you go back to her apartment, is that what you did? In which case you've got a hell of a nerve coming in here and grabbing me as though you've been lost in the jungle for ten years!"

A slow smile spread across Josh's face. "You're jealous."

"I'm not! I just don't like you going straight from her to me like that."

He said carefully, because he couldn't betray Sharon's confidence, "She and I went to the bar at Harbour's Edge, talked for half an hour and then went dancing. I took her to the lobby door of her apartment building and came straight home."

"Oh." She glowered at him. "Home, eh? You're only renting part of my house, that's all you're doing—don't you go calling it home."

"Clem, I'm staying here at least three months, and I'll call it what I like!" He took a deep breath. "We always end up angry with each other, don't we? Here we are are fighting over what name I give my apartment."

She managed a faint smile. "It's called a power struggle," she said. "I'm used to having my own way and so are you. Therefore we fight."

"And who do you think will win?"

"I own the house—I will."

"I wasn't talking about the house," Josh said softly.

Momentarily Clem looked disconcerted; but only momentarily. "Unless you choose to use brute force—and I would suspect that with you that would go against the grain—there'll be no more kisses by the coat stand."

"There's all the rest of the house."

"The day of the caveman is over."

"True. It's been replaced by the day of the twentieth-century woman. Feel free to take the initiative with me any time you want, Clem."

"Another reason we fight is because you won't take no for an answer," she snapped. "Water wearing down a stone—is that how you get your women?"

"I've never found it necessary before." Wanting to leave her off balance, he dropped a quick kiss on the tip of her nose, said, "Well, this has been a most interesting and instructive half hour, but I need my beauty sleep. Good night, Clementina," and headed for the stairs.

By a very strong effort of will he managed not to look back. And on Sunday he went jogging again.

He also stayed right out of Clem's way on Sunday and indulged in some concentrated thought. In the long weeks he had spent in jail he had gradually come to recognize his need to settle down in one place, marry and raise a family; to do so involved finding a wife. He had had a shadowy picture of a pretty brunette, someone not unlike Sharon, bright and intelligent and fun to be with. Clem did not fit that picture. Clem was not at all shadowy. She was a tall, full-bodied woman who walked with the pride of a lion and had strong opinions on almost everything.

Clem did not want to get married, and she was certainly afraid of sexual involvement. With him, at any rate.

He was a fool to waste his time on her. He was thirty-three years old, and his father wanted grandchildren. Josh was not a conceited man, but surely there must be women around who'd be happy to have him for a husband. So why hanker after a stormy-eyed woman who had hated him when she was ten and did not seem to have ameliorated that position very much in the intervening years?

Furthermore, he was deluding himself to attach cosmic significance to an embrace in the hallway at two o'clock in the morning. He was sex-starved, that was all. He was eating better, putting on weight, exercising again; why should he be surprised that his sexuality should also be coming to the fore?

Perfectly natural. Clem had a ripe, mature figure and they were sharing the same house. Of course he would be attracted to her; there'd be something wrong with him if he weren't.

But he didn't have to take her to bed, and he certainly didn't have to marry her.

He reached this conclusion about four o'clock in the afternoon, called Sharon and suggested they go for a walk and have a pizza downtown, and pushed Clem firmly to the back of his mind. On Tuesday he and Sharon went shopping for a new sofa for her apartment, and on Wednesday he had a blind date with Pete's next door neighbor, the one who was divorced; her name was Xanthia, and as soon as she came to the door he saw that she was every bit as exotic as the name suggested.

She was also, unless he was totally misreading the signals, willing.

They went to see *Driving Miss Daisy*, a movie she loved and he found pleasant; in the foyer they bumped into a group of her friends and had rich desserts at a little restaurant near the cinema, during which the friends, all heavy smokers, convivially blew smoke into his face; when he drove Xanthia back to her town house, she invited him in for a nightcap. He was curious to see how a living space identical to Pete's would reflect her personality, so he accepted.

Xanthia favored jarringly bright colors, art so abstract as to be meaningless, and the kind of furniture into which one sank and had difficulty resurfacing. She poured Josh a very generous brandy of excellent quality, turned on a single lamp, low, and put a sultry-voiced singer on her tape deck. She then arranged herself seductively beside him in the depths of the sofa—with an ease that bespoke practice—and started playing with his ear, first with her long red fingernails, then with her lips.

They kissed; she had most certainly studied the Kama Sutra. His senses should, perhaps, have been reeling. They were not. Her perfume was cloying, her bracelet was tickling his ear, and his brain remained distressingly clear. He knew he would regret it in the morning were he to avail himself of Xanthia's charms; nor was it just that she was too practiced. Something else was wrong; something that rankled in the back of his mind but that he could not articulate. He therefore extracted himself with as much poise as he could muster, and drove home.

The downstairs of Clem's house was ablaze of lights. It was eleven-thirty on a week night and Clem had to work the next day. Josh's heart slammed against his ribs. Something was wrong.

He had never covered the ground between the car and the front door so quickly. The key turned smoothly in the lock and he burst in the front door. "Clem?" he yelled. "Are you okay?" And only then did it occur to him that he was going to look an awful fool if she was with Douglas or Jamie or the stodgy lawyer.

"I'm in the kitchen," she called.

He hurried down the hall. She was kneeling on the floor holding Armand in her arms, her long legs in faded jeans, her hair pulled back in an untidy ponytail, and in one of those flashes of insight that Josh had learned to ignore at his peril he realized he had not ended up in Xanthia's bed because Xanthia was not Clem. It had been that simple.

He said urgently, "What's wrong?"

As she raised her face, he saw that she had been crying. "It's Armand—he's sick. I called him to come in before I went to bed, you know how he loves to be outdoors, and he was okay then. But he didn't jump up on my bed as he usually does, and when I came out here five minutes ago, he was like this."

Gently Josh touched the cat's black nose; it was hot and dry, and Armand was panting in distress, his belly distended. "Have you phoned the vet?"

"Just before you got here. She'll be at the clinic in fifteen minutes, I was just about to call a cab."

"Find something to wrap him in and we'll go right now."

She neither argued nor thanked him; in a way he found obscurely flattering, she seemed to take it for granted that he would help her. They drove to the clinic and in half an hour Armand was being operated on for a hernia. Clem had elected to stay until the operation was over; she prowled up and down the waiting room, her hands in her pockets, her shoulders a tense line. Josh was sitting down, pretending to read a magazine. The waiting room had harsh fluorescent lighting and the chairs had not been chosen for comfort.

As though she couldn't stand the silence, Clem said, "I know he's only an animal, he's not a person, and after some of the things you've seen in Africa you must think I'm a silly sentimental female to get so upset over a cat, but——"

"I don't think that, Clem."

"—but I love my cats and I hate to see them suffer."

Her voice wavered and tears began trickling down her cheeks. Josh could not stand to see her crying; it hurt something deep within him. He put down the magazine, got to his feet and said, "Come here."

She looked at him defiantly. "I'm not crying, not really." Then her face crumpled. "And you've got lipstick on your ear," she wailed, "I noticed it as soon as you came in the kitchen."

When Josh lifted his hand to his face and scrubbed at the skin by his ear, his fingers came away fuchsia. Crossing the tile floor, he looked her in the eye and said loudly, "Nothing happened. Nothing, Clem."

"It's nothing to do with me if it did," she said, rubbing her eyes with the back of her hand.

Josh was no longer so sure about that. "Nor, just to keep the record straight, was I with Sharon," he added.

"You do get around, don't you?" Clem said nastily.

"Like someone else I could mention," he replied and grinned at her. "We're not going to have a fight here. I'll get you a Kleenex."

He passed her the box off the counter and watched as she blew her nose and dried her eyes, small prosaic actions that filled him with compassion. She muttered, "I must look awful."

The end of her nose was red and her cheeks were blotched. "Ravishing," Josh said solemnly.

Her lips twitched. Josh said on impulse, "You really hated me when you were a kid, didn't you, Clem? I know I was the one who told you what was going on between my father and your mother... was that the reason? Or was there something else?"

He had her full attention; Armand was, at least temporarily, forgotten. She said with spontaneous truth, "Before that day you told me, I worshiped the ground you walked on—you were the knight in shining armor, Paul McCartney and Tarzan all in one. You were also five years older and dating every girl under the sun... but I figured I'd grow up and get rid of my braces and then you'd notice me."

"Instead of which I dumped all my anger about our parents on you and then became your stepbrother."

"Well, yes . . . it all seems a very long time ago."

"And in the meantime you have grown up and gotten rid of your braces."

"If you're implying that you're finally noticing me, you're nearly twenty years too late," Clem said with a tight smile.

"Not as far as I'm concerned . . . even ten years ago would have been too soon, because I was wandering around the globe and you were getting your education." He paused, wanting her to understand. "That spell in jail was a real watershed for me—there's nothing like several months of enforced solitude to make you think. Assess your life and see what's really important. I know what I want now, and I won't settle for less."

"Just don't make it me!"

"I'm not sure that I have," he said slowly, "But——"

The inner door opened and the vet said, "Clem?"

Clem's head swung round. The vet, gray-haired with a kind face, said, "Armand's fine, we got him in time. I'll keep him for a day or so, and then you can take him home."

Clem's shoulders sagged, and tears flooded her eyes again. "Thanks," she gulped, "thanks so much."

"If you want to go out the front door, I'll lock up behind you," the vet said briskly, and nodded good-night to Josh.

He drove Clem home, hung up her coat in the hall and said, "You'll be exhausted tomorrow."

"No date tomorrow night—I'll go to bed early." She added straightforwardly, "Thank you, Josh, I really appreciate all your help."

He was very much aware of the two of them being alone in the house; he wanted to kiss her so badly that it was a physical effort to keep his hands by his side. "You're welcome," he said. "Sleep well."

She suddenly reached up and deposited a kiss as light as the wings of a butterfly on his cheek. She then blushed entrancingly, opened her mouth, said nothing, and closed it again. Turning on her heel, she almost ran down the hall to her own rooms. Josh, feeling as though the sun had burst through a cloud, watched her disappear into her bedroom and heard her close the door.

Did that wisp of a kiss mean that she was finally starting to see him as a man? No longer as a brother? No longer—and how he had hated that phrase—as a safety valve?

CHAPTER FIVE

ON THURSDAY morning it was raining, a steady May downpour. Clem had left for work by the time Josh woke up, and that brief kiss in the hallway no longer seemed quite so meaningful in the dull light of morning. He listened to the water drumming on the roof and decided he would buy a membership at one of the university gymnasiums today. If Clem were to be unavailable, he could at least lift weights. And he did have a date with Sharon this evening.

When he was ready to pick Sharon up for the ballet, Josh watched until he saw Clem walking along the street before heading down the stairs. He was being manipulative and mean of spirit; but he was damned if she should think she was the only one to go on dates.

Slipping his trenchcoat over his new gray pinstriped suit, he unlocked the front door. Clem was climbing the steps. She looked tired. Josh said casually, "I'm glad I bumped into you—what's the word on Armand?"

"Eating and drinking and quite unappreciative of all that's been done for him," she said. She looked him up and down, her expression unreadable. "You're very smart."

"Sharon and I are going to the ballet."

"I see. Duncan and I are going tomorrow. Because he's on the board of the symphony we're invited to the reception as well."

It was unlike Clem to be catty. She must be tired, thought Josh, and hardened his heart. "We'll have to compare impressions on Saturday...is it a date?" he

78

said, and, not waiting for an answer, ran down the steps. "See you later."

Clem was still very much in his thoughts when he pressed Sharon's buzzer; but Sharon was so patently looking forward to the evening, her vivacious face set off by a pretty flowered dress, that he put Clem to the back of his mind. They had a wonderful meal at a restaurant by the waterfront, and each enjoyed the ballet, Sharon preferring the more traditional numbers, Josh the more modern. They went for a drink afterward, and only then did Sharon ask, "Big date with Clem on Saturday night?"

"No. Any word from Jamie?"

"No." She stared into her rum and Coke. "I really like you, Josh, but I'm not the slightest bit in love with you."

He patted her hand. "I feel the same way about you...although it's too bad we couldn't fall in love, it would tie up all the loose ends, wouldn't it?"

"So have you got plans for Saturday night?"

"Play with the cats? Swim fifty lengths of the pool? In other words, no."

"Would you like to come with me to my parents' farm? They live outside Wolfville, about an hour's drive from the city. Not a sophisticated place, but they'd make you very welcome. I'll be leaving Saturday morning."

Josh didn't even hesitate. "I'd like that, Sharon, thanks," he said, touched. Until Sharon had spoken, he hadn't realized how little he wanted a weekend alone in his apartment, with nothing much to do except keep track of his landlady's various dates. "I thought I'd offer to pick up Clem's cat at the clinic, but I could do that first thing in the morning."

So on Friday evening about seven Josh went downstairs. The ballet was at eight; Clem should be almost

ready. As he was about to call her name from the bottom
of the stairs, she came out of the bedroom, and the words
stuck in his throat. Her black dress had exquisitely simple
lines, baring the creamy length of her throat and her
hollowed collarbones as well as rather a lot of leg, contrasting sharply with the rich mane of her hair and the
wide-set gray eyes. Her earrings were massed black beads,
her tights opaque black, clinging to her legs. In one hand
she was carrying a pair of high-heeled black shoes. She
gave him an impudent grin. "Do I pass?"

He nodded, not sure he could find his voice. She had
dressed up like this for Duncan, he thought, and felt a
highly unsettling mixture of jealousy, envy and hurt
churn inside him.

She twirled around, obviously delighted with herself.
"I'm really looking forward to tonight, I love ballet."
Then she plucked at the skirt of the black dress. "Do
you think Duncan'll guess what I paid for this?" she
asked.

Josh cleared his throat, hating the fact that she had
spent a lot of money to impress a man who was un-
worthy of her because he had none of her zest for life.
"It looks expensive."

"Ten dollars at the secondhand shop on Sydney
Street." Clem gave a rich chuckle. "I only hope the
original owner isn't at the ballet, that's all."

Some of Josh's depression lifted. "Will you tell
Duncan what it cost?"

"Not likely! Like Queen Victoria, he would not be
amused . . . did you want something, Josh, by the way?"

He had almost forgotten why he had come looking
for her. "I was going to suggest I pick Armand up at
the clinic for you tomorrow morning."

"That's all right, Jamie's coming here at ten-thirty to
take me there. Thanks anyway."

It was bad enough that, looking good enough to eat, Clem was going to the ballet with Duncan; that she should be spending time with Jamie when Sharon would have given her soul to do so was ten times worse. Josh was suddenly and illogically furious, illogically because he knew it was not Clem's fault: if Sharon was to be believed, Clem was ignorant of any connection between Sharon and Jamie. This, however, did nothing to abate his anger. "You cover all the angles, don't you?" he said unpleasantly. "The rich boyfriend to take you to the ballet—and the reception, let's not forget the reception—in a Mercedes; the widowed football coach to help out with the cats and God knows what else; the nice safe medical student for week nights so you can exercise your maternal instincts. And it all allows you to stay as emotionally uninvolved as—as that coat stand. Congratulations, Clem!"

"I'm not like that!" she cried. "How dare you? You make me sound so cold-blooded and detached. As if I'm using them for my own ends. I wouldn't do that. They're my friends—a word you apparently don't know the meaning of."

For an instant an image of a quiet, blood-soaked clearing flashed across Josh's mind. He said with deadly calm, "Don't you talk to me about friends...I'm talking about something else altogether. You're scared to death some man might touch your heart, might force you into taking the kind of emotional risks the rest of the world takes every day—so you flit from one to the next, playing them off against each other, and never letting any of them near enough to be any danger. And I'm quite sure if one of them is foolish enough to fall in love with you you get rid of him so fast you can't see him for dust."

Clem was white with fury. "Do you know what your problem is—you don't like me doing precisely the same thing that you've been doing for the past ten years. If a man decides he doesn't want to get married no one thinks anything of it, he's just another bachelor—which is hardly a pejorative term—a dashing and romantic figure. But if a woman pushing thirty doesn't want to get married she's called a spinster, she's on the shelf, poor dear, and men like you think they have the right to label her neurotic for what in a man would be a perfectly reasonable and defensible decision.''

She had run out of breath. Josh said flatly, "Great red herring, Clem. Talk in generalities, bring in one of society's many double standards and thereby deflect Josh from the personal. And if you can make him feel guilty at the same time, all the better. Very clever! Every word you said is true: there's an immense bias in our culture against the single woman, and when you and I go out for dinner together we can have an interesting and productive discussion on that subject. But not right now. Because I don't want to talk generalities. I'm talking about you. And me. Two specific people in a specific situation——''

"The only situation I'm in is that I'm going to be late for the ballet," Clem interrupted furiously. "And I'll never have dinner with you—never!"

"Why not? Because I might upset the nice tidy little apple cart you've made of your life?''

"Get lost, Josh," she seethed, and bent over to pull on her thin-strapped shoes, her jerky, uncoordinated movements infinitely seductive to the man watching her. As she wrestled with the tiny buckles, she added, "A good rousing fight—what a great way to start the evening. Thanks a lot.''

Ignoring her sarcasm, his jaw set, he said, "When are you going to quit running, Clem?''

She straightened, now almost as tall as he, twin scarlet patches staining her cheekbones like the makeup of a clown. "You're like Brad," she choked. "You can't stand anyone saying no to you. Get this into your head, Joshua MacNeill—I shall behave exactly as I please, and just as soon as the three months are up you'll be out of here so fast the neighbors won't even see you go."

Josh disliked being compared to Brad just as much as she must have known he would. The truth is, he thought, that I can't stand *you* saying no to me. He then abandoned thought for a move that was strategically less than wise but that expressed his frustration precisely. He seized her by the black sleeves of her dress and planted a kiss full on her mouth.

It was a thorough kiss. It was also a thoroughly angry kiss. Clem reacted by wriggling strenuously and by kicking him on the shins with the pointed toes of her shoes; the first excited him, the second hurt. He let go of her and said, "Admit it, Clem—you'd have much more fun at the ballet with me."

Her response was predictable. "But you've already been," she said with a nasty smile. "With Sharon."

That she was absolutely right did nothing to allay Josh's anger. He opened his mouth to speak, but before he could say anything Clem added haughtily, "Excuse me, please, I have to finish getting ready," and walked away from him down the hall. Her hips swayed in the narrow black skirt; he clenched his fists and watched her go.

She had won that round, he decided, clamping his jaw shut so that he wouldn't call after her. His emotions were still boiling inside him like lava in a volcano, and the top most were easily labeled: rage, frustration and desire. His strongest urge, he thought with coruscating honesty, was to pick her up bodily and carry her to his bed and make love to her as she had never been made love to before. Not by any of her men.

As Clem with deliberate restraint closed the bedroom door gently behind her, Josh fought to control himself. Scratch the surface of the civilized man, he thought grimly, and the primitive emerges. None of the women he had ever known had made him feel like this; he was not even sure he liked feeling like this. For, under the confusion that raged in body and mind, he was aware of fear. A sick fear that in itself made him even more afraid.

Maybe Clem genuinely didn't want anything to do with him. Maybe she didn't even like him.

When his father had married Arabella, his mother—his cool, self-contained, career-oriented mother—had been shattered. Josh at fifteen, forced to cope with adult emotions he was ill prepared for and which had frightened him by their rawness and intensity, could remember her saying in despair, "It takes two people to make a marriage, Josh—one person can't do it on his or her own. Your father doesn't want to be married to me any longer. There's absolutely nothing I can do about that."

Equally, Josh thought now, standing in the hallway and hearing the distant sounds of Clem moving around in the bedroom, it takes two people to build a relationship. He couldn't do it on his own. Not if Clem didn't want him.

Duncan's going to be arriving any minute. Do you want him to find you standing in the hallway lusting after the woman he's taking to the ballet?

With an impatient exclamation Josh ran upstairs to get his jacket and his car keys and left the house. As he turned the corner at the end of the street a beige Mercedes swung into the street; Josh caught a glimpse of a black bow tie against a white shirtfront and said several swear words in a very loud voice. He then headed downtown. He'd buy himself the best steak the town could offer and go to a movie. What he was not going to do was sit around meekly waiting for Ms. Clementina Delaney to come home from the ballet!

However, by nine o'clock Josh was home again. The list of movies had not inspired him, so he had gone to an appliance shop and bought himself a VCR and then to a video shop where he had browsed along the shelves and picked out *The Unbearable Lightness of Being*; he'd read the book several years ago and enjoyed it. Once home, he borrowed one of Clem's screwdrivers from the basement and started setting the machine up, during which he nearly deafened himself before he figured out the volume controls. But eventually the copyright law imprinted at the beginning of the film started sliding past on the screen. Josh pushed the stop button and straightened, pleased with his new purchase. He'd pour himself a drink before he settled down, and he'd return the screwdriver.

He was walking into his kitchen when he heard, very softly, the sound of a door closing downstairs.

He stood still, his ears straining for any further sounds. Nothing. But he had not imagined the slight squeak of hinges or the click as the latch slipped into place. Someone was in Clem's part of the house. And it wasn't Clem, for she was at the ballet in a sexy black dress. With Duncan.

Josh grinned wolfishly to himself, slipped his feet out of his deck shoes and padded toward the stairs, the screwdriver still clutched in his hand. He was in the mood for a little action. Whoever was down there was going to be very sorry he'd broken into Clem's house.

He took the stairs one by one, avoiding the boards that squeaked, and was on the bottom one when he heard another muffled sound from the bedroom. Adrenalin surged through his veins; every sense on the alert, he crept across the hall carpet, tucking the screwdriver in the pocket of his jeans as he went. He paused outside the door, then, in a blur of movement, flung the door opened and burst into the room.

Clem screamed.

It was a very loud scream that echoed in Josh's ears. He said foolishly, "It's you!"

She sat down hard on the bed and said shakily, "You scared me out of ten years' growth . . . *what* do you think you're doing?"

Josh had had long enough to recover his wits. "Apprehending the person who'd broken into your house while you were at the ballet," he said.

"I'm not at the ballet. As you see."

She was wearing jeans and an old sweatshirt and her feet were bare; a pair of wispy black stockings dangled over the arm of her chair while the black dress lay abandoned on the bed. She took a brush out of the evening bag that was also on the bed and began yanking it through her hair, her expression far from friendly.

"I know you weren't stood up because I saw Duncan come to get you," Josh said slowly. "So what's going on, Clem? Are you hiding him under the bed?"

"When you moved in three weeks ago, we talked about privacy," Clem said in an ominously quiet voice. "Kindly allow me mine by going back upstairs and minding your own business."

He leaned against the doorframe, crossing his legs and regarding her quizzically. "Give, Clem—I'm the one you can confide in, remember?"

"I don't want to!"

"Oh, come on, tell big brother Josh all about it."

She glowered at him. "All right, then! The reason I was creeping around in my own house like a common thief was so you wouldn't hear me. I feel," she compressed her lips as she sought for the right word, "humiliated."

"You told Duncan the price of your dress and he declined to escort it to the best seats in the house."

A reluctant smile curved her mouth. "Well, no, it wasn't that." She sighed, then said in a rush, "I got a phone call from Muriel Brownlee just as he arrived. Muriel enrolled her daughter Jenny in the daycare this week—she's new in town, doesn't know a soul, no money, no job. Jenny was struck by a car this evening, and Muriel was phoning from the emergency department; they were operating on Jenny and she was nearly out of her mind with anxiety."

As Clem raised troubled eyes to Josh's face he interposed, "So you went there to see her, and Duncan went on to the ballet?"

She nodded unhappily. Josh looked at his watch. "Get dressed and I'll run you to the arts center—you'll still be in time for the reception, if nothing else." He was a damn fool delivering her into another man's keeping, especially in that black dress, but he knew how much she'd been looking forward to the evening.

She said tightly, "As soon as I made it clear I had to go and sit with Muriel for a while, Duncan phoned his mother and took her instead. He was—upset."

"Bastard," said Josh.

Clem blinked. "I'll have you know his antecedents are impeccable."

"His antecedents may be. His manners aren't."

She added gloomily, "The ballet's sold out for tomorrow night."

"Clem," Josh said rashly, "the next time the ballet's in town, I swear on a stack of Bibles I'll take you."

"You'll probably be married to Sharon by then."

"Even if I have ten wives, I'll still take you to the ballet."

She looked minimally less depressed. "We could all go together," she said, "all twelve of us, in procession. And I hope Duncan—and his mother—are there to watch."

Josh grinned at her. "Only one condition. That you wear that black dress."

She laughed. "It's a very tight fit. I'll have to cut out chocolate chip cookies." Then she added with a wry smile, "Thanks, Josh...*you* understood why I had to go to the emergency department, didn't you?"

"You wouldn't have enjoyed the ballet if you hadn't. Tell me how Muriel and Jenny are."

"They had to set Jenny's broken leg under anesthetic, and she had multiple bruising. But she'll be fine. Muriel just needed someone to hold her hand while she waited, and once we saw the doctor she was okay."

Josh was suddenly visited with the strong conviction that Judy, Pete's partner, would not have given up the best seats in the house beside an important lawyer to sit with a mother on welfare in a hospital waiting room. Judy would have gone to the ballet. He said sincerely, "You're a good person, Clem."

She looked embarrassed, as though his compliment had knocked her off balance. "Oh," she mumbled, "not really."

"And," he went on with a wicked grin, "here you are dateless on a Friday night—you can't expect me to pass that one up. I bought myself a VCR this evening, and I rented *The Unbearable Lightness of Being*. Why don't we watch it together?"

She looked at him suspiciously. "We're not going to start dating each other," she said. "That would spoil everything."

Josh said with absolute truth, "I don't have any intention of becoming one of your boyfriends, Clem."

Nor did he. If he couldn't be the only one, he wouldn't be one at all. All or nothing, he thought. And with a strange tug at his heart knew he would much prefer it to be all.

"Okay, then." She brightened. "Why don't we make popcorn? You can't watch a movie without popcorn."

"With melted butter."

"And lots of salt. All the things that are bad for you." She bounced off the bed. "I bought new popcorn last week."

Twenty minutes later they were settled side by side on the couch in Josh's living room, a large bowl of buttered and salted popcorn between them. Josh pushed the play button and the movie started.

The very first line that Tomas, the hero, spoke was to one of his mistresses. "Take off your clothes," he said. And she complied. The next scene was with his other mistress Sabina, bewitchingly sensual in a big bowler hat and her artist's smock, who also undressed for him, revealing lacy black lingerie and a pliant, seductive body. Her hair tumbled to her shoulders. Tomas shed his clothes. They began to make love, slow, practiced love that was plainly for the pleasure of the act itself.

Acutely aware of the woman at his side, wishing he had chosen any other movie than this, Josh munched on the popcorn and wondered if Clem had been wearing black lingerie under her dress. With her tawny mane of hair and her ivory skin, she would look exquisite in black lace.

He felt a stirring in his loins and tore his thoughts away from her, considerably relieved when the scene shifted to the hotel where Tomas met Tereza, who would become his wife. But there were more lovemaking scenes as the movie continued, and through his own discomfort he realized how Clem had shifted further away from him on the couch and was sitting with a rigid stillness that spoke volumes. She was no more comfortable than he was; although, being a woman, she did not have to worry about any obvious outward signs.

The movie eventually ended, a bittersweet ending that Josh had anticipated from his memories of the book. He flipped the video to rewind and reached for the bowl of popcorn at the same time as Clem, so that their hands brushed. She jerked hers away and the bowl lurched toward the edge of the couch. Josh grabbed at it. "How did you like the movie?"

"It was fine," she said in a brittle voice, not meeting his eyes. "Longer than I'd expected—I'd better get to bed."

She reached for the bowl. Josh held on to it and said, "Clem, I——"

"Give it to me!" she demanded, and suddenly between them raw sexual tension flared into hostility.

His answer was to take her by the elbows, push her back into the pillows and kiss her with a desperate craving that in some dim corner of his brain horrified him.

He would have expected her to fight him tooth and nail. Instead she wrapped her arms around his neck, almost choking him, and kissed him back with a fierce passion. He half fell on top of her, the fullness of her breasts crushed to his chest, their legs entangled in a way that inflamed his senses. As he braced a knee on the side of the couch, her tongue flickered against his lips and in an explosion of desire he knew he wanted this woman

as he had never wanted a woman before. His tongue
darted to meet hers and they kissed with a frantic and
ever deepening hunger.

Then Josh brought his hand to Clem's breast, cupping
its softness and warmth, the nipple hardening to his touch
through her sweater in a way that made him groan deep
in his throat. A shudder rippled through the supple body
pressed to his, making him forget all caution. He fumbled
for the waistband of her shirt, thrusting his hand beneath it to find the silken smooth skin and the racing of
her heart under the swell of her breast.

Clem dragged her mouth away from his. "Josh, no—
please, no!"

Her eyes were distraught, filled with terror where moments before they had been filled with passion. His
breath rasping in his chest, Josh levered himself up on
his palms. "Did I hurt you? Clem, I'm sorry——"

"No, you didn't hurt me, but you must stop," she
cried incoherently. "I don't know what came over me
to behave like that, I never do, I must have been mad..."
She bit her lip, looking on the verge of tears.

He sat up, pulling her upright, smoothing the hair back
from her face then taking her hands in his; she suffered
his touch, her lashes hiding her eyes. He said strongly,
"Sane, not mad. Sexual desire is a perfectly normal in-
stinct. We want to go to bed together——"

"No, we don't! It was because of the movie, that's
all it was; I *won't* go to bed with you, Josh, I won't."
She was trying to tug her hands free, as terrified as a
wild animal in a trap.

Josh let her go and stood up. The turmoil in his body
was gradually subsiding but his brain was racing. Clem
was not acting; her terror was genuine. As genuine as
those few, heart-stopping moments of passion had been.
And he did not understand either one. He watched in

silence as she picked up the bowl of leftover popcorn, which miraculously had not spilled, and clutched it to her chest. "Good night," she gasped and left the room with undignified haste.

Josh gazed after her, his brow knit. Passion and terror. What did it mean?

The farm that Sharon's parents owned overlooked the long red peninsula called Blomidon, and the tidal waters of the Bay of Fundy. The sunsets were spectacular, the meals delicious and the welcome warm; outwardly, at least, Josh relaxed. But within him the tension stayed coiled like a snake that would strike at the slightest provocation; he carried Clem with him as he and Sharon tramped across the fields herding the cows, as they washed dishes at the sink and played card games with her family.

He never mentioned her name in front of Sharon's family, nor did Sharon ever mention Jamie's. But as Josh drove back to Halifax he felt as though there were four people in the car, he and the dark-haired woman beside him, Clem with her mane of curls, and six-foot, obdurate Jamie. He kissed Sharon on the cheek when he left her at her apartment and thanked her warmly for the weekend, then drove home.

Jamie's car was parked in the driveway.

Early Saturday morning, out of a motive of common politeness but also flattering himself that Clem might worry if he did not come home that night, Josh had left Clem a brief note on the table in the hall, saying he would be at Sharon's parents for the weekend. He now bitterly regretted his punctiliousness, for all of Clem's men Jamie was the one who threatened him most. Perhaps Clem had used his absence as the opportunity to have Jamie stay all weekend.

His imagination promptly presented him with a graphic image of the two of them in bed.

His thoughts raced on. He knew from personal experience that Clem was a passionate woman; perhaps Jamie did not frighten her as he, Josh, did. Perhaps Jamie had been the one to slake that passion.

He parked his car by the curb and turned off the ignition. What the devil was happening to him? How in only three weeks had a contrary woman with toffee-colored hair turned his life upside down? He had come here to find peace. To recuperate. Instead of which he was sitting in his car watching his hands tremble on the wheel and not sure whether it was rage or pain that like a hungry lion was tearing him into pieces.

He forced himself to take several deep breaths. He told himself it was none of his business what Clem did on the weekends. He gripped the wheel until his knuckles ached and the trembling stopped. Only then did he get out of the car, reaching for his overnight bag on the back seat.

But as Josh walked up the path the lion walked with him, and it took all his courage not to turn around, go back to his car and drive away. Adding to his struggle was another layer of betrayal: the house itself had betrayed him. The welcome it had offered him had been an illusion; it had brought him anything but peace. With an almost paralyzing reluctance he approached the steps. He'd go straight upstairs, he'd pour himself a strong drink and turn the volume on the television to maximum, and tomorrow if he was smart he'd look for somewhere else to live.

The front door opened and closed, and Jamie crossed the porch and started down the steps. When he saw Josh he stopped dead on the third one down. He was wearing sweat gear and a ski jacket, clothes that suited his well-knit body; his strong-boned face was immobile. Slowly he descended the last two steps.

Josh let his bag drop to the ground and made no effort to mask his aggression. "And how was your weekend?" he said.

"Fine," Jamie said, clipping off the word. "I saw your note. You spent the weekend with Sharon."

Jamie, who was now standing level with Josh, was perhaps an inch shorter; although Jamie had not spent four months in a prison cell suffering from malaria and dysentery. In a reckless surge of belligerence Josh said, "And you spent it with Clem."

"I did not."

"I know you were taking her to the vet's yesterday morning and I know you're just leaving her place Sunday evening—what the hell else would you call it?"

"I don't give a damn what you call it, I did not spend the weekend with Clem!" Jamie's jaw jutted out pugnaciously. "You putting the move on Sharon?"

"What's it to you if I am?" said Josh.

He felt like a ten-year-old squaring off in the school yard; he felt wonderful. Because all his senses were keyed to their highest pitch, he saw anger flare in Jamie's blue eyes, and then reason clamp down on it. Ruthlessly he pressed his advantage. "You told Sharon a year ago you didn't want involvement and you've been dating someone else—Clem—ever since. What right have you got to complain if Sharon spends the weekend with me or with anyone else?"

"None," Jamie said tightly.

Josh might be angry, but he was not so angry that he couldn't recognize fellow-suffering when he saw it. He said more moderately, "Jamie, Sharon'll probably kill me for this, but I'm going to say it anyway. She's eating her heart out over you. Has been for the last eleven months. When are you going to do something about that? Or do you even want to?''

Jamie said in a voice from which he had removed all emotion, "You wouldn't be stringing me along, would you?''

"I am not."

"Even though you've just spent the weekend with her."

With a twinge of regret Josh felt the last of his anger evaporate. "I like Sharon very much, and she likes me. We're neither of us the slightest bit in love with the other and never will be, and don't ask me to explain that, because I can't. Nor have I done anything but kiss her on the cheek."

Jamie's stolid face did not change expression. "When I saw your note on Saturday morning I felt as if half a dozen linebackers had just landed in a heap on top of me—don't laugh, man, I mean it. You see, I figured I'd forgotten Sharon. She was someone I met too soon after my wife died and so I quit seeing her . . . best thing for both of us, I thought, even though I knew I hurt her at the time. I didn't like seeing the two of you at Pete and Mindy's party, but that was just a party, that wasn't the same as spending the weekend together." He hesitated, running his finger around the neckline of his shirt. "Are you saying if I called her up she'd go out with me?''

"She sure won't if you don't," Josh said acerbically, remembering the pain in Sharon's big dark eyes.

"Yeah . . ." said Jamie. "You got a point there." A grin split his face; he made a couple of imaginary passes at Josh, bouncing lightly on the balls of his feet. "I've never been to bed with Clem," he said generously. "She made it clear from the start that that wasn't on the cards, and that was fine with me, it's what had got me into trouble with Sharon. Clem and I are buddies, Josh. No more, no less." He gave Josh a considering look. "I don't think she liked that note any more than I did."

Trying to subdue the intense flood of emotion that Jamie's words had brought him, an emotion that in a rather cowardly way he was calling relief, Josh said, "Now you're stringing me along—go and call Sharon."

Jamie dropped his fists. "What happens if she won't speak to me?"

"She will," said Josh, who was by no means sure she would.

"You know what? The toughest player I've got is six-foot-six, two-fifty pounds, and I'd rather face him any day than Sharon. I'm not scared of him."

Josh laughed, suddenly liking Jamie very much. "Just don't take her for granted."

"You kidding?" Jamie made another of those lightning-swift feints. "Tell you what, if Sharon and I get it together, the four of us'll go out together. Sharon and I, you and Clem."

"Clem wouldn't date me if I was the last man on earth."

"You ever asked her?"

"I don't——"

From the front porch Clem said suspiciously, "Is something wrong, Jamie?"

Josh's head swung around; she did not acknowledge his presence. Jamie gave a comical grimace. "I never told her about Sharon," he said to Josh in a melo-dramatic whisper.

"You deal with Sharon," Josh said. "I'll look after Clem."

Jamie gave him a quick punch in the chest. "Thanks, man," he said, waved his hand in Clem's general di-rection, and headed for the gate. Josh climbed the steps. "Hello, Clem," he said.

She glared at him. "What were you and Jamie talking about?"

"Sharon."

Her voice dripping with sarcasm, she said, "I do hope you had a nice weekend."

As Jamie backed out of the driveway in a squeal of tires the full impact of that beautiful word "buddies" finally struck home to Josh. Clem had never made love with Jamie; she had not wanted to. He did not need to be jealous of Jamie.

Intuitively he had always been sure she and Douglas were not lovers; or she and Duncan. Which left Manuel. He said bluntly, "Clem, have you ever made love with anyone?"

Her lashes flickered, and for a split second he was sure he had his answer. Then she said coldly, "What *did* you and Jamie talk about?"

"I told you—Sharon. She's in love with Jamie and I suspect Jamie's in love with her. Although he's been too scared to admit it."

Clem's jaw dropped. "He's never even mentioned her name to me—are you *sure*?" Josh nodded. Agitated, Clem exclaimed, "I never would have gone out with him if I'd known that!"

"I know you wouldn't, Clem."

Patently hurt, she said, "So in the week you've known Sharon you've found out more than I have in the year Jamie and I have been friends."

"Men aren't brought up to talk about their feelings."

"That's true enough," she snorted. "When I looked out the window the two of you were squaring off like a couple of prizefighters."

Josh grinned. "Things were a little tense for a while. He didn't like me spending the weekend with Sharon. I didn't like him being here with you. How's that for an honest feeling, Clementina?"

"You don't have any claim on me," she snapped.

"None whatsoever."

A gust of wind blew across the porch, and she shivered. Josh added, "We could discuss our putative love life inside in the warmth rather than on the front porch."

"There's nothing to discuss."

"We could discuss what we did on the weekend instead. Over a cup of tea in the kitchen."

Clem shot him a fulminating look. "One thing about you, Joshua—you're persistent." She opened the door, stalked into the hall and said ungraciously, "I'll put the kettle on."

It was not a date. But it was better than nothing. And Clem, unless he was very much mistaken, was a virgin.

The discussion of the weekend was stilted and short-lived, for Clem's mind was obviously still preoccupied with Sharon and Jamie; Josh soon went upstairs to his own rooms, although he first, casually he hoped, found out the time of Clem's lunch hour at work. He was not discouraged by the rather perfunctory nature of their conversation, for Clem's terror of him on the couch on Friday night was now taking on far more interesting connotations.

He put a match to the wood in the fireplace and sat in the nearest armchair watching the flames. Clem for years had assiduously avoided sex, for sex invited intimacy and intimacy commitment. Clem did not believe in commitment, and had the glaring example of Arabella to prove her point. She had managed very well with this policy until he, Josh, had come back into her life.

Clem, no more than he, could be blind to what happened between them whenever they touched each other. Call it chemistry, call it lust, call it physical attraction...the label didn't matter. The pull was there, fierce and powerful and undeniable. Clem felt it; and it frightened her out of all proportion, because it threatened the house of cards she had so painstakingly constructed ever since she had grown into womanhood.

Therefore Clem was determined to keep him, literally and figuratively, at arm's length. Friday night had been her only slip. On Friday night the Clem she was capable of being had all too briefly escaped. He knew it. Worse, she knew it.

Because of Friday night, if he were to ask her for a normal date, like dinner and dancing at a nightclub in town, she would date ten football coaches rather than go with him. So he had to come up with an alternate strategy. One that would work. One that would get past her defenses. Because, he thought, watching a shower of sparks shoot up the chimney like miniature fireworks, Clementina Delaney was becoming very important to him.

Was he in love with her? During the long dark hours in prison he had fashioned a mental image of love as golden sunlight drenching a field full of wildflowers...peaceful and secluded and very beautiful. What he had felt so far was tumultuous jealousy, the primitive assertion of his loins, and great waves of anger shot through with disconcerting moments of tenderness. Did all this add up to love?

He had no way of knowing. What he did know was that he would not rest until he understood more fully the mystery that was Clem. Until she was naked to him, body and soul.

CHAPTER SIX

MONDAY morning was windy and crisp and clear, just the day to implement step one of Josh's strategy. He left the house about eleven, spent an enjoyable half hour in a toy shop, and then drove to the Mother Goose Daycare Center, arriving five minutes before Clem's lunch hour. When he walked in the door, he saw Clem right away; she was holding Robin in her arms, three more children were clustered around her knees, and she was laughing. Instantly he imagined her with their first child in her arms, the child of their love, and in an actual physical shift felt himself bound to her more strongly than before.

"Hello, Clem," he said, and his voice sounded strange in his ears.

When she saw him, she put Robin down. Robin instantly waddled over to Josh and said hopefully, "Dad, Dad, Dad." Josh bent and picked him up. "Hello, there," he said, and watched Clem edge free of the rest of the children and walk over to him; he had no idea whether she was pleased to see him, indifferent to his presence, or was about to show him the door. Indifference would be the worst, he thought, and said, "Are you free for the next hour?" She nodded cautiously. "Good! Grab your coat and let's go."

"Where?"

"You'll see. Come along."

"I'll have to tell Louise I'm going."

"Hurry up, then." He played peek-a-boo with Robin while he was waiting, and once she reappeared he distracted Robin with some blocks lying on the floor, helped

Clem on with her coat and hustled her out of the door. When he was seated beside her in the car he said, "We're going to Citadel Hill to fly a kite and I have sandwiches for you in the back seat." Quickly he pulled away from the curb.

Amusement warming her voice, Clem said, "How did you know I love kites?"

"I guessed."

"Think you're pretty smart, don't you?"

"Some days more than others," Josh said agreeably.

He drove up the hill to the granite fortress that since the eighteenth century had guarded the city, and parked the car. On the grassy slopes below the road he handed Clem the kite. It was a great writhing dragon with yellow eyes and a long green tail, and it took to the air with a leap, straining at the cord in her hands. Josh took a turn ten minutes later, then Clem again; then they wound it in, and ate their sandwiches in the car.

Clem's cheeks were pink from the wind, and she chattered away with none of the constraint of the night before. When Josh took her back to the daycare center with five minutes to spare, she turned to him, wind-tousled, still laughing. "Thanks, Josh, that was really fun."

He kissed the tip of her nose, which was also pink. "Any time," he said, and drove off well pleased with himself.

That evening, half an hour before Douglas usually arrived, he went downstairs to find Clem. "In the kitchen," she called. She was crouched on the floor with a cat he had never seen before, a very fat cat with long gray hair. "I'm looking after him for my friend Nicola," she said. "His name is Major. Armand seems to like him but Rosebud is being very snooty. I do hope he'll settle in all right."

Josh wanted to take her and Major into his arms. That's not step two, he thought. Keep your head, Josh. Instead he asked, "Clem, have you got any painting you'd like done? I'm putting out feelers on a new job but I'm taking at least another month off, and painting is one of those pleasantly mindless tasks that seems to suit the way I feel right now."

She sat back on her heels and said shrewdly, "What are you up to, Joshua MacNeill?"

"The day before I moved in I talked about doing some odd jobs for you. Making amends, isn't that what I called it?"

"That was nearly a month ago...why this sudden urge now?"

He pulled a chair out and sat down, resting his feet on the table. "It's part of my new strategy," he said amiably, amused by her perspicacity. "If I ask you for a regular date you'll turn me down, and I don't like rejection any more than the next guy. So I'm attempting the oblique approach."

"Kite flying. Painting the dining room. What next?"

"If I told you, it wouldn't take you by surprise."

She tried to look severe and failed. "I can't imagine why you want to date me—I haven't been very nice to you."

"I'm not sure either," Josh said honestly. "I just know I do. But painting the dining room will be fine for now. Pick out a color and I'll get the paint."

"I already know what I want." Clem rummaged in a drawer near the sink and produced a color card. "White semi-gloss latex trim, and this green for the walls. Flat latex. I thought the green would be nice with all my plants." As he studied the card, she added, "If you do this for me, then I'll feel indebted—is that part of your strategy?"

"Give me credit for a little more subtlety than that."
She said in a low voice, "You scare me, Josh."

Deliberately he kept his long body relaxed in the chair.
"I know I do. I'm trying very hard not to."

"But you'd like to be in bed with me. Right now."

"Of course."

"Josh, you could paint fifty dining rooms, and I might
still not do that."

He brought his legs down to the floor and stood up.
"Don't worry about it," he said. "If it happens, it will
happen naturally, because we both want it. If not—well,
I'll dig up your entire garden and take up marathon
running...and now I'd better get out of here before
Douglas arrives."

"Are you planning on picking up the slack from
Jamie?" she asked, hurt lingering in her voice.

"I'm not going to pick up the slack from anyone,"
Josh said emphatically. "When you're ready, you'll make
time for me...leave out some old cloths so I can cover
the furniture in the dining room, okay?" and he went
upstairs.

He enjoyed himself the next day, filling in and sanding
all the cracks in the plaster, and edging the windowpanes
with tape. Then he showered and at five o'clock was
waiting for Clem outside the daycare center. She ran
down the steps at five past, saw his car and stopped.
Then she slowly walked over to him. He rolled down the
window on her side. "Want to go out to Peggy's Cove
and see the surf? Gale force winds last night and this
morning."

"How do you know I don't already have a date?"

"You're going to turn him down for the sake of my
blue eyes." He added with low cunning, "I bought two
pieces of chocolate cake from the bakery."

She opened the door and got in beside him. "Ah... you've finally found the way to my heart."

They talked all the way to the fishing village, whose brightly painted wooden houses were perched on huge granite rocks scraped bare by glaciers; a tall white lighthouse on the promontory overlooked an ocean lashed to fury. As Josh got out, zipping up his rain slicker, the wind tore the car door from his fingers, and the crash of the waves and the hiss of flung spray assaulted his ears. He grabbed Clem's sleeve. "Let's go over on those rocks," he yelled.

They struggled down the slope against the gale, then clambered up a steep rock face to a lookout a safe distance from the water. Josh stood behind Clem, pulling her back against his chest, looping his arms around her waist to hold her steady. The power and energy of the sea, the roar of the wind and the thud of the waves on the rocks took his breath away. As he braced his legs, Clem's hair tickled his chin. She was pliant in his arms; but only, he thought, because he was insignificant in the face of such fury.

She twisted around to point out a spectacular wave rearing out of the sea. He gripped her more tightly as it raced toward its collision with the rocks, a collision that shot out a starburst of spray that hung in the air, then collapsed, to hiss in white streamers across the gray granite. Clem laughed back at him, licking the salt from her lips with unselfconscious zest.

Josh forgot all his good intentions, all his resolve not to frighten her as she had been frightened on Friday night. With a strength that seemed part of the sea's violent energy, he pulled her around to face him and kissed her, a kiss that made no attempt to mask the force of his desire. He wanted her. He wanted her more than breath itself, and the heat of his mouth and the slide of his tongue on her salt-stained lips told her so. As another wave thudded on the rocks, he realized with a shock of amazement that she was kissing him back every bit as fiercely, opening to him, pressing her body against his and digging her nails into his wet hair.

He strained her to him in a passion of gratitude and need, seeking the sweetness of her mouth, murmuring her name, his mouth burning a trail from the delicate softness of her throat to the taut line of her jaw and along her cheekbone. Then she pulled his head down again so that their lips met and sealed and melted together; he thought his heart would slam its way out of his chest.

The wind shifted, driving needles of spray into Josh's face; instinctively he recoiled, and Clem clutched his shoulders for support. He found himself gazing straight into her eyes, gray eyes drowning in the same desire that had claimed him, and when he lifted his hands, tracing the straight dark brows, the arc of her lids, the generous sweep of her forehead, his fingertips lay claim to her, taking possession. Her skin was wet to the touch, her hair clinging to her scalp, yet she had never looked so beautiful to him. There were no words to say. He bent his head, letting his kiss say all that was in his heart.

The wind buffeted them. The spray soaked through his jeans. He ached to hold her body, swathed in the shiny folds of her red raincoat, and with the remnants of his common sense knew this could not possibly be the time or the place. Then he felt her hands, cold and clammy, slide under his slicker and his sweater to find the bare warm skin of his back. He shivered from pleasure and surprise, and felt her jerk them away.

He smiled into her eyes. "Put them back, I'll warm them for you."

Her cheeks pink from more than the wind, Clem obeyed, with a mixture of shyness and boldness that entranced him. "You're freezing," he teased, sensing that the slightest wrong move on his part would send her back into her shell.

She suddenly flattened her palms against his flesh, chuckling as he winced at their chill. It was a small gesture that seemed astonishingly intimate to Josh; because his body was so unmistakably giving the message that he wanted her, he eased away from her. In quick alarm she said, "Don't you like me doing that?"

"If you didn't have a such a thick coat on, you'd know exactly how much I like it."

She blushed scarlet and said helplessly, "Oh, Josh, what are we doing?"

"We're being honest," he said. "Honest about the way we react to each other. That's all." He smiled at her. "You're quite safe. I shan't suddenly fling you down to the bare rock and haul off your clothes. We might scare the sea gulls."

As though the wildness of their surroundings precluded anything but the truth, she blurted, "I don't act like this with anyone else I know—I've never wanted to. To the point where I've wondered if there was something wrong with me."

"You must learn to trust in the way you feel when you're with me," Josh said soberly. "That's all that's wrong."

In sudden tension her fists clenched under his sweater. "You make it sound so easy."

"It doesn't have to be difficult, Clem."

She made a quite undecipherable sound somewhere between humph and pshaw, and said, "Let's go home, I promised Louise I'd drop over for tea after supper."

She was protecting herself, Josh knew. She was also worth waiting for; for if Clem could free herself from fear, he could not imagine a more generous and passionate lover than she would be.

He wanted her, yes. He had probably wanted her from the first time he had seen her striding along the road, singing to herself off-key. But more than that, he wanted her to be free.

First thing the next morning Josh painted the dining room ceiling, and when it had dried in the afternoon he did all the edging on the walls with a brush. He then poured paint into the tray he'd bought and started with the roller. It was very satisfying work, and he liked the green Clem had chosen; his favorite rendition of *La Traviata* was on the radio, turned up loud enough to hide the lapses in his own voice as he sang along; he'd do the woodwork tomorrow morning, he thought, and then he and Clem could move the furniture back the next day. Beautiful Clem...at the top of his voice he accompanied Alfredo in declaring his undying love for Violetta.

Then, through a sixth sense he had depended on for months, Josh suddenly knew he was being watched. As he tensed, someone touched him on the shoulder. He whirled, automatically assuming a defensive posture, the roller held in front of him, his other arm braced to meet an attack.

Tiny splatters of paint dribbled down the front of Clem's shiny red raincoat. She had shrunk back from him, her eyes appalled. As Alfredo's voice trailed into silence the violins echoed in an exquisite diminuendo.

Josh dropped his arms and said flatly, "Oh, hell."

Clem swallowed. "I—it looks very nice," she said.

He put the roller back in the tray, picked up a clean cloth and said, "Here, let me wipe your coat... Clem, I'm sorry, I didn't hear you coming, and I guess I've spent enough time in rough-and-tumble places in the last few years that I've learned to react first and ask questions afterward. I didn't mean to frighten you."

He stooped to catch a trickle of paint near the hem. She said with a careful lack of emotion, "It's more to do with the prison than with anywhere else, isn't it? You told me they mistreated you there."

There was no more paint on her coat. Josh stood up, moving his shoulders uneasily. "It was mostly when they were bored and didn't have anything better to do."

"But you had to defend yourself as best you could."

He grimaced. "At odds of six to one, I learned to move fast."

Clem put her handbag down on the floor and flung her raincoat over the nearest dust cloth; her rust-colored jumper and pristine white blouse made Josh very aware of how much green paint seemed to have ended up on his hands and his clothes. Then she stepped closer to him, rested her hands on his shoulders and kissed him on the mouth.

She was not quite as confident as she looked, for the first touch of her lips was questioning. But she must have felt his shudder of pleasure, for she joined her arms around his neck and kissed him with more assurance, and in a dizzying surge of delight he felt the shy slide of her tongue. As he opened to her, his heart thudding in his chest, he found time to wonder if he were dreaming. And then he lost track of time altogether...

When Clem eventually moved back from him, her eyes were full of confusion and her cheeks were flushed. He said dazedly, "I'll paint the whole house if you like."

"I—I don't know why I did that."

He grinned crookedly. "Perhaps because I can't hug you back. Not unless you want to end up moss green."

"So I'm quite safe—just as I was on the rocks." Mischief lit up her face. "Close your eyes," she said.

He obeyed, standing very still, and knowing with absolute certainty that being with Clem made him happier than he had ever been in his life. She kissed him again, this time with an unbridled if unpracticed sensuality that made his senses reel; then she slid her hands down his chest, exploring through his thin cotton shirt his leanness, the ladder of his rib cage, the flatness of his belly, concave to his belt. There her hands stopped.

Josh opened his eyes. Immersed in his own quickened breathing and the throb of his arousal, it took all of his willpower to keep his arms slack at his sides. Bringing her hands to the base of his throat, Clem tested the racing pulse and traced the hard line of collarbone. Then she lifted them to his shoulders, molding the muscles and feeling in them the rigidity of tension, the outward sign of his inward struggle for control. She bit her lip. "I'm being unfair," she said. "I don't mean to tease, Josh."

"I love everything you've done," he said. "And it's all right—I promise you won't end up with paint all over you."

"So you'll hold back for my sake...because I'm afraid." He nodded, watching her frown in concentration. "Did you learn your self-control in prison? Or have you always had it?"

"Not always, no. Each day in that hole in the ground was an exercise in frustration and fear, and I had to learn to cope with that—I'd have gone mad otherwise."

She shivered. "It's another world, isn't it, so far from this one? Yet you'll always carry it with you."

"Don't feel sorry for me, Clem," he said harshly.

"I'm not," she said levelly. "But if I'm to get to know you, I have to understand how that whole experience has affected you."

She had stepped back from him. Josh took a long slow breath and said, "Do you want to get to know me?"

Again she bit her lip. In a low voice she said, "I want to make love with you. Some time."

He knew that for her this was a huge admission. He said gently, "You have a lot of stability in your life, Clem—your house and your job and your friends. Even your male friends. I'm the only one who represents risk, aren't I?"

"Once you've done something you can't go back."

"You may not want to."

"Maybe." But she did not look convinced.

He said with deliberate lightness, "Why don't you give me half an hour to finish this wall and have a shower, then we could order a pizza for dinner? I'll pick it up if you want to order it."

"Okay," she said, and moved another step back to pick up her coat. "That would be nice." Then she scurried out of the room.

Josh dipped the roller into the paint and went back to work. His strategy was working beyond his wildest expectations.

He finished the dining room the following morning. After supper Clem waxed the floor and Josh cleaned the windows; they then replaced the furniture. They were arguing amicably over whether the sideboard was centered against the wall when the front doorbell rang. Clem looked puzzled.

"Douglas? Duncan? Manuel? Brad?" Josh said. "I could continue."

"No need for that," Clem said primly, and went to answer the door. A couple of minutes later she ushered Jamie and Sharon into the dining room.

Jamie's usual phlegmatic features were suffused with happiness and—Josh as a fellow male recognized the signals—sexual satiation. Sharon looked radiant. She gave Josh an unselfconscious hug and said, "We've come to say thank you, Josh. Because you brought Jamie and me back together."

Jamie took his hand in a bone-crushing grip. "Thanks, man," he said. Then he turned to Clem. "I reckon I owe you an apology for never telling you about Sharon—I figured it was all behind me, and no point in talking about it."

"You're forgiven," Clem said, kissing him on the cheek, then hugging Sharon. "And I'm glad you're both so happy. I think this calls for a glass of wine."

They toasted each other, the dining room, and the arrival of spring, then Sharon said, "We want to take the two of you out for dinner, as our guests—on Saturday if you're both free?"

Clem looked discomfited. "Paul's company is having a reception for the directors on Saturday, and he asked me to go with him. You could go without me."

"Nope," said Jamie. "The following Saturday?"

She looked at Josh, and he could read her mind as clearly as if she were speaking. This was a real date. This was not flying a kite or watching the surf or painting the dining room. "All right," she said.

Josh raised his glass. "To risk," he said, "without which life has no savor."

Clem blushed, Jamie gave Sharon a rather too explicit kiss, and Josh realized that his much vaunted self-control was not going to last much longer.

* * *

On Saturday Josh went grocery shopping with Clem and
took a detour to the orchid show at the museum on the
way home. The colors were vibrant and some of the
blossoms, in Josh's eyes at least, flagrantly sexual. He
gazed at a pink and white bloom, lipped, frilled and
grooved, and decided he had sex on the brain. He did
not share this insight with Clem.

However, after he had dropped her off at the house
to get ready for her date with Paul, he went to the
pharmacy. Clem and he were going to make love soon,
he told himself, frowning at the appropriate display
counter and hoping to God that he was right. If and
when they did, he wanted to be ready.

That evening he went to Pete and Mindy's for dinner,
and once the baby was settled they watched the video
of *Moonstruck*, a love story with a happy ending.
Afterward Josh drove home and went to bed, which he
was sharing with Major the cat, who seemed to have
taken up residence in Josh's apartment. Josh had grown
fond of Major in the last few days, but it was Clem he
wanted to share his bed with, not Major.

Clem came home shortly after midnight. At two-thirty
Josh was still awake. He had come to the conclusion
that next Friday he was going to get a reservation at a
country inn with a king-size bed and a Jacuzzi; he'd fill
the room with roses, he'd provide champagne on ice,
firelight and poetry. And if he couldn't persuade Clem
to join him there he was no kind of a man. Painting
dining rooms was all very well, but he wanted more, and
so did she. And it would be better if they were out of
the house, on neutral territory. No telephone, no cats
on the bed, no boyfriends ringing the front doorbell.

He turned the pillow for the tenth time and closed his
eyes. He was almost asleep when he heard, distantly, the
tinkling of broken glass.

He stared up at the ceiling, not sure if the sound had been real or part of a dream. Then he heard another sound, like the scrape of wood on wood, followed by a faint thud. Moving very quietly, he got out of bed. This was no false alarm: Clem had not made those noises.

His paint-spattered jeans were draped over the chair. He pulled them on, not bothering with a shirt or shoes, and padded across the bedroom to the hall.

Clem screamed, a sharp cry of fear that was suddenly cut off.

Josh covered the hall carpet in two long strides and leaped down the stairs three at a time. He heard something crash to the floor, heard another bitten-off cry and a smothered curse. Her bedroom door was open. He burst in and as if there were a camera in his brain taking a snapshot of the scene he saw the empty bed with the clothes dragged almost to the floor, the smashed lamp against the wall and two figures struggling on the carpet: Clem, kicking and scratching, her pale green nightgown ripped from hem to thigh, and on top of her a man in black. Then Josh saw the light catch on the blade of a knife, and like lightning he struck.

He knew a number of very dirty moves that he had picked up in places as diverse as Port Moresby and Cairo, and he used every one of them. In less than two minutes Clem had been rudely shoved aside and her assailant was lying flat on his back on the carpet, bleeding quite profusely from the nose, his eyes shut. The man on the carpet was, not to Josh's surprise, Brad.

Josh was also bleeding from a shallow wound in his arm; ignoring it, he pulled the cord from Clem's housecoat and tied Brad's hands behind his back. He then knelt on the carpet beside Clem and put his arms around her. "Did he hurt you?" he said urgently.

She shook her head, burrowing it into his chest; her whole body was shaking, and she was breathing in tiny shallow gasps. He rocked her to and fro, rhythmically stroking her back, and said, "He must have broken a window, I heard the glass break...I'll call the police in a minute. It's okay, Clem, just as long as he didn't hurt you."

"I was asleep," she muttered. "Then all of a sudden he was on top of me, I thought I was dreaming, and then I saw it was Brad and I s-screamed." She shuddered, her hands convulsively clutching Josh around the waist. "He put his hand over my mouth, so I bit him and then somehow we fell on the floor..."

"Along with the lamp," said Josh.

"I was trying to reach it so I could hit him with it—it all happened so fast and then I saw his knife and I was so afraid...thank God you heard, Josh."

Brad stirred, then rolled over, his eyes opening. He shook his head, said something unprintable, and strained against the cord binding his wrists. Clem flinched away from him.

Josh pulled her to her feet. "You go in the kitchen and call the police." His voice hardened. "I'll stay here with him."

Although she was swaying on her feet and her face was paper white, she said, "He'd better behave, because you fight awfully mean, Josh MacNeill." Then her eyes widened. "Oh, Josh, you're hurt——"

"It's just a scrape. Off you go, Clem."

There was a note in his voice that he rarely used; she went. A moment later he heard her talking on the phone. Brad had pulled himself up to lean against the foot of the bed, and was swearing in a monotonous undertone that Josh purposely blanked from his mind; he knew that a murderous anger was boiling just under the surface of his self-control, and that as long as he lived he would never forget Clem's terrified, bitten-off scream.

Clem came back in. "They'll be here in a few minutes," she said from the doorway, carefully avoiding looking at Brad. "I want to get dressed, Josh—would you pass me my clothes?"

Her jeans and a sweater were lying across the chair. Josh handed them to her and she vanished in the direction of the bathroom. By the time the police came she had washed her face and brushed her hair, although she was still pale; she told her story in a composed way and led them into the kitchen where a litter of broken glass lay on the floor and a cold draught came through the broken window. Josh added his bit, Clem signed a statement, and Brad was led out of the front door to the waiting police car. Lights flashing, it drove off.

Josh locked the front door and said, "Why don't you make some hot chocolate—it seems to be the best antidote for these middle-of-the-night escapades, doesn't it? I'll get a board and some nails and close the window off."

In a small voice she said, "I'd like a hug first."

She went into his arms with the trust of a frightened child. He held her closely, and only after a minute or two did he realize she was crying, her tears trickling down his throat and landing on his bare chest. "I kept thinking about your friends," she gulped. "The ones who died. I realized tonight how quickly it can happen—when I saw Brad's knife I really thought I was going to die."

He felt a red-hot rage rise in his throat again, and knew it was just as well that the police had taken Brad away. "I'll sleep on the couch in your living room for the rest of the night," he said. "It'll make you feel safer."

"I'm not usually such a coward."

"You're not a coward at all—you'd have to be a fool not to have been frightened tonight."

"I'll never go to a rock concert again," she sniffled.

She sounded more like the normal Clem. Josh patted her on the shoulder and said, "Hot chocolate, Clementina."

By the time he had picked up the pieces of the broken lamp, made her bed and then nailed a board over the kitchen window, she had made the chocolate. She put his in front of him and then plunked a first-aid kit on the table as well. "Sit still," she said. "I'm going to clean up that scrape on your arm."

"That's Douglas's field, not yours."

"I have first-aid training because of the daycare, you've got dirt in it from the carpet and it's my turn to give the orders—so stop arguing and sit still."

She sounded very fierce. Josh subsided, wincing a little as she washed the grit from the abrasion, applied an antiseptic cream and then two sterile pads, which she taped into place. "There," she said, "that's better."

The gentleness with which she had worked, the way she kept her tongue clamped between her teeth in concentration, the well-remembered scent of her hair had all worked their magic. Josh took a handful of her hair and drew her face down, kissing her mouth. "Thanks," he said.

When she shivered in sudden panic, he knew she was remembering Brad. Not quite sure how to handle this, he said lightly, "I'm Josh. Not Brad."

"Sorry," she mumbled, and took a big gulp of hot chocolate. The light was shining on her right cheekbone, already bruised where Brad had hit her. She was right to be afraid, he thought; he, as a male, could easily be seen as the enemy.

This was a far from comfortable thought. Josh drained his mug and said abruptly, "I'll get the covers from up-stairs and bunk down on the couch. See if you can catch up on your sleep, Clem."

She pushed herself up from the table. "I'd rather you slept with me," she said.

For several seconds of dead silence Josh could think of nothing to say. He was almost sure she meant the word sleep in the literal sense. Almost. "All right," he said, trying to disguise the uncertainty in his voice.

"I've spent lots of nights alone in this house and I've never been afraid before," Clem said in a rush. "Just for tonight, Josh. Even if it's only until daylight."

She quite definitely meant it in the literal sense. And after what had happened tonight, he could not possibly press for anything else and still live with himself in the morning. How's that for a test of your self-control, Josh? he thought mockingly and said, "I'll go up and get a pair of sweatpants—I don't own pyjamas."

"Oh." She swallowed. "Okay."

Upstairs Josh changed into gray sweatpants and a T-shirt, noticed that Major had deserted the bed for his sweater drawer, and turned out the lights. When he went into Clem's room she was standing by the bed clad in a long flannelette nightgown that left uncovered only her hands, her head and her feet; she looked as though she were already regretting her invitation. He said calmly, "Which side of the bed do you want? I won't eat you, Clem."

She blushed. "This side, please."

He walked around the other side of the bed and climbed in, turning his back and pulling up the covers. "Does that give you enough room?"

"Yes, thank you," she said as politely as if she were at a tea party.

She turned off the light by the door, and the mattress shifted as she joined him in the bed. She appeared to be as far over on her side as she could be. Grimly Josh closed his eyes, trying to blank out of his mind everything but the lateness of the hour and his need for sleep. Several minutes passed.

With a tiny thump one of the cats jumped up on the bed. Clem sat bolt upright with a gasp of sheer terror. "*Josh* . . . oh, God, it's Rosebud."

Josh rolled over, said, "Come here, Clem," and pulled her down into his arms.

She huddled into him, her head butting his chin. "This is ridiculous, I'm a nervous wreck," she moaned. "The cats sleep with me every night—what's *wrong* with me?"

"Dearest Clem," Josh said forcefully, "Brad didn't break in here to play parlor games. He had rape on his mind. You know that as well as I do. You should be afraid, you have every right to be afraid, and right now I'm less than proud to be a member of the male sex. But one thing I'll tell you—as long as I'm living in this house no one, but no one, will frighten you like that again."

He sensed her listening to him very intently. She mumbled, "I guess for the last two hours I've been avoiding that word. Rape."

"It's a horrible word." He smoothed her hair with his hand. "Have you ever taken any courses in self-defense?"

Against his chest she shook her head. With a thread of laughter in his voice he went on, "Then my advice is to drop Paul and Manuel and even a couple of the others and take karate instead, and no, that is not totally disinterested advice."

"Christine gave me the same advice, actually, the day Brad came to the daycare center. And hers was disinterested. I could practise on you. And you could teach me a couple of those things you did to Brad.''

"They aren't in the book," he said dryly. "Feel better?''

"Much."

She lay still, her breathing slow and even. She had draped one arm over his hip, with an innocence that touched him to the core, and her fingers were loose and relaxed; he thought of Xanthia's practiced and artificial skills and would not have exchanged Clem's virginal bed for one of them.

Clem gave a long sigh. Her body twitched. She slept.

Josh forced himself to immobility, certain that he would never be able to fall asleep with Clem so close. The next thing he knew it was daylight, and a song sparrow was chirping outside the window. Armand was lying in the crook of his knees and Rosebud at his feet; Clem, in the night, had turned over, so that her back was now curled into his chest. She was deeply asleep.

One of his arms was snug into her waist. The other, under her, was pressed into her breast.

It would have been very easy to begin stroking her body, to have smoothed and kissed and coaxed her into submission; and he was almost sure she would submit, and do more than submit. Welcome him. Join with him in passion and delight. But somehow he wanted their first lovemaking to be played differently. He wanted Clem to take the initiative. In broad daylight to walk willingly into his arms, knowing exactly what she was doing, free from all her old fears. He didn't want to sneak up on her in the night.

You're a fool, Josh. Too much nicety of conscience.

A fool he might be. Nevertheless, he very carefully edged his arm free and drew away from her. She murmured something in her sleep, then turned on her back, and her breathing resumed its slow, even rhythm.

He reared up on his elbow, reluctant to leave her, studying her sleeping face with secret pleasure. Her nose had a tiny bump in it. Her chin, even in sleep, was firm; Clem, he thought with a wry smile, knew her own mind. Except where he was concerned. Her mouth was soft, infinitely kissable.

Grimacing, Josh eased himself out of the bed. Armand yawned at him, Rosebud ignored him, and Clem slept on. He crept out of the room and went upstairs to his own bed, where Major mewed a welcome from the drawer, and where within ten minutes he fell asleep again.

CHAPTER SEVEN

JOSH woke to the distant chime of church bells and to a nearer, more mysterious sound, a combination of mewling, purring and tiny squeaks. He rolled over, frowning, remembering all the various events of the night. The house, apart from Major's contribution, was quiet. Clem must still be asleep.

The sounds were originating from his sweater drawer. Hitching up the waistband of his sweatpants, he stood up and looked in.

Major, in the night, had given birth to three tiny kittens. Squirming, blind, pink, they were curled into the cat's belly. Major blinked up at Josh and purred all the louder.

Josh's new blue sweater, the one that matched his eyes, would never be the same again. Josh sat down on the bed and began to laugh.

Then he glanced at his watch. Ten to eleven. Time he woke Clem up and told her a few basic biological facts.

A couple of minutes later he was tapping on her half-open door. He heard her murmur something sleepily, and walked into her room. She was curled into the pillows, the two cats still keeping her company, her hair even more tangled than usual. Suppressing some very strong libidinous impulses, Josh said cheerfully, "Good morning. How did you sleep?"

He could trace her return of memory: shock and fear, with embarrassment close on their heels. "I didn't hear you get up," she said, pulling the covers well up to her chin.

"I didn't intend you should." His eyes dancing, he said, "Your turn to get up, Clem—I've got something to show you."

She looked at him with narrowed eyes. "Not another break-in?"

"Not my etchings, either. Although it is upstairs in my bedroom." He suddenly chuckled. "And it is a rather basic lesson in sex."

"Just how gullible do you think I am?" she demanded.

He laughed out loud. "Actually, very gullible."

"What *are* you talking about?" she said, and he was glad to see the strain was leaving her face. "Give me five minutes."

Josh waited by the newel post in the hall, and in a couple of minutes Clem joined him, belting her housecoat around her waist. He was obscurely pleased she hadn't got dressed, for it seemed to say that she trusted him. He should broach the subject of Friday night to her today, he thought, leading the way up the stairs and already feeling his nerves tighten at the prospect; for it was entirely possible that, poetry and the Jacuzzi notwithstanding, Clem would say no.

He led the way into the bedroom and said, "Next time your friend asks you to keep her cat, you should find out how many cats she means." Then he stood aside so she could see the open drawer.

She gave him a puzzled look as Major mewed. Then she hurried across the room past his unmade bed and peered into the drawer. "Oh, Josh," she breathed, clasping her hands in delight, "aren't they sweet?"

As she knelt down by the drawer Josh joined her on the other side of it, she watching the cats, he watching her. Her face was a study in wonderment and awe at the miracle of birth; her emotions were entirely unselfconscious and straight from the heart. Josh remembered her holding Robin at the daycare center. He pictured her holding their own child at her breast. And straight from his heart came the knowledge that he loved this woman in a way he had never loved a woman before, for he was bound to her body and soul and would be until the day he died.

He felt as though Brad had hit him over the head. He felt as though he had won a million-dollar lottery. He felt exalted and humbled and happy and grateful. He also felt scared.

It was perhaps not altogether a fortuitous time for such a discovery. When Clem looked up, her luminous gray eyes met his undoubtedly dazed blue ones and she said sharply, "Are you okay?"

Josh had enough presence of mind to realize he couldn't possibly tell her of his discovery, for, if at some level he was frightened by it, she would be appalled. "Yeah...yeah, I'm fine," he muttered, dragging his eyes away and focusing on the purring cat in the drawer. "You'll have to call him Majorette."

"I prefer Marjorie," Clem said. "These are the first kittens born in the house since I bought it . . . they're darling, aren't they?"

"Darling," Josh said, and this time looked her right in the eye.

Clem blushed scarlet, reached a tentative hand partway across the drawer and just as quickly tried to withdraw it. But Josh was too fast for her. He took it in his own, raised it to his lips, and slowly, lingeringly kissed her palm. When he felt her other hand very lightly caress his hair, he let his lips drift up to her wrist, where he found the pulse fluttering beneath the blue-veined skin, skin that was as smooth, as delicate as the finest silk, yet as warm as if the sun had shone on it. He pushed her sleeve back, burying his face in the softness of her inner arm, feeling his heartbeat thicken and pound in his chest. And his breathing catch in his throat.

Her arm came around him, pressing his head to her breast. "Josh," she breathed, "oh, Josh..."

Clumsily he edged around the drawer and pulled her into his lap, cupping her face in his palms and seeking her mouth with his own, finding there the bewitching mixture of shyness and passion that seemed to epitomize Clem to him and that every time he had kissed her had bound him to her more strongly. He caught her lip between his teeth; as she opened to him, he tasted the sweetness of her mouth while at the same time his hands began exploring the long line of her spine and the curve of her waist. Tugging at her belt, he loosened the folds of her housecoat and stroked her belly up to the full, taut breasts. And there, suddenly, he stopped.

Drawing back, he said huskily, "I want to make love to you—right here, right now." He spared a glance for the carpet on which they were kneeling and eased a crick in his knee. "Although I guess we could move up to the bed, it would be more comfortable. Clem, I'll protect you against a pregnancy, and I'll be as gentle and as careful of you as I can. But if you don't want to make love, if you're not ready, then now's the time to stop—if we go any further, I won't be able to."

"My choice," she said gravely.

He nodded, forcing himself to keep his hands at his sides, trying to school his face to immobility. Then she smiled at him, although her lower lip was quivering very slightly, and stood up, reaching a hand down to him. "I think we should move to the bed," she said.

He had his answer. Joy rushed through Josh's body as strong as an ocean wave. Letting her pull him to his feet, he slipped the old blue housecoat from her shoulders and started undoing the pearl buttons at the throat of her flannelette gown. "That's a very sexy nightdress," he said seriously. "Do you wonder that I'm driven mad with lust?"

"If you were a true romantic, you would have made the bed," she retorted, her laugh a little unsteady.

There were two dozen buttons, each of which slipped and slithered through his fingers as he tried to force it through its loop. "I'd planned a big seduction scene at a country inn for this Friday night. Roses, champagne and candlelight."

"We could still do that... providing I like being seduced."

The unsteadiness was now in her voice. Josh said quietly, "Oh, you'll like it, Clem...I swear you will. There, that's the last one."

He hauled his T-shirt over his head, then swung her into his arms and put her down on the bed. As he joined her there, the springs creaked ominously and Major broke into a purr like a drum roll. Clem gave an unexpected, rich chuckle. "Candlelight, roses and no cats?"

And then she said nothing else for several minutes, for the simple reason that Josh was kissing her with all his newly found love and with as much skill as he could muster. Afterward he was never quite sure how he extracted Clem from the folds of the flannelette gown or when he stripped off his sweatpants; what he did remember with aching clarity was the first sight of her naked body lying beside him on the rumpled sheets, the endless, slender length of her legs, the narrow waist, the full, creamy breasts, rose-tipped.

He spoke the literal truth. "You take my breath away."

"Truly?"

A note in her voice caught his attention. He said, "I'm no poet—I was going to depend on Shakespeare for the great seduction scene—but you're more beautiful than I could ever have imagined."

"Oh." She wrinkled her nose endearingly. "I've often felt there was too much of me—that it would be fun to be one of those tiny fragile women with big blue eyes."

"They terrify me," said Josh. "I like you exactly as you are." And with hands and lips he set about convincing her just how much he did like her. The result was a gathering whirlwind of passion, interspersed with whispered intimacies and with moments of laughter because they were unused to each other and hence awkward and because Clem had never made love before and seemed to have little idea of what to expect.

She might be innocent, thought Josh, watching her face as he teased open the warm wet petals between her thighs, petals that reminded him of the orchids, but she was also generous and full of courage and quite transparent in her pleasure. She liked everything he did and she was not afraid to show it. And as passion claimed her, she flung away her inhibitions, running her fingers down his body from chest to thigh, discovering with open wonderment the heat and throb of his arousal, kissing him so wantonly that he almost lost control.

Almost. For he could not bear to hurt her, and so with every nerve in his body and with infinite patience he tried to ensure that she was as ready for him as she could be before he entered her. She was whimpering deep in her throat from the slide of his fingers on her flesh, her hands clasping his hips with a strength that further excited him when he finally lifted his weight on his palms, his eyes seeking in her flushed cheeks and frantic eyes the confirmation he needed.

Then, with a pleasure so sharp it was almost pain, Josh felt her guiding him into her. He bit his lip, overwhelmed by the primitive need to thrust and claim for his own the writhing, glorious body of the woman underneath him. As though she had been fashioned for him alone, she gathered him in, and then he saw, even in the extremity of raw hunger, the flash of pain, sudden and sharp, splinter through her desire. He held himself still, his arms trembling, and said hoarsely, "Clem...am I hurting you?"

She took him by the buttocks and moved her hips and the pain vanished from her face, her features blurring instead with a naked longing that was the only signal he required. He let go of his control, thrusting into the dark throbbing center of her, hearing her cry out his name and from a long way away hearing his answering cry that was both anguish and victory, and yet something more as well: a spiraling into a depth of emotion that for want of a better word was called love.

His arms could not hold him any longer. He collapsed on top of her, and against his wrist felt the frantic racing of her heart. He wanted to tell her he loved her, and that, because he loved her, this had been an experience unlike any other in his life. The words were on the tip of his tongue, for they were the right words, the words that belonged to this coupling and to this woman; but he bit them back.

Gradually the rasp of breath in his throat slowed. He eased his weight off her and murmured into her tangle of hair, "Clem . . . are you all right?"

Her drowned gray eyes were level with his face on the pillow. She said helplessly, "I didn't know that making love would be like that—so devouring. So impossible to resist. So incredibly powerful."

Josh put an arm around her waist, drawing her closer so that her breath stirred on his cheek. "The more you give, the more you receive, Clem. You were wonderfully generous.''

''*You* were just plain wonderful.'' She ran her fingertip down his nose and said, ''You have little dark flecks in your eyes and your hair is so so soft...'' She added with naive pleasure, ''I never knew what a man felt like, Josh, and now I do.''

''Any time,'' he said.

''You'll have to give me five minutes to recover.'' The laughter faded from her eyes. ''I have no experience to fall back on, but I have the feeling that you, too, were generous, and that you were watching out for me every step of the way. Thank you, Josh.''

He could not tell her he loved her but he could kiss her with all the tenderness that the words implied. He did so, tasting afresh the sweetness of her lips and catching the musky scent of his own body on hers. ''Do we have a date for a country inn with a fireplace on Friday night?'' he murmured.

''Yes, please. Providing you don't forget the poetry and the Jacuzzi.''

''Or the roses...so you like being seduced, Clementina?''

''Oh, yes,'' she said with such fervor that they both burst out laughing. She then looped an arm across his ribs, kissed the hollow at the base of his throat and closed her eyes with a sigh of pure contentment. She was asleep within minutes; Josh lay still, wondering not altogether facetiously if one could die of happiness.

He must have slept himself; he woke with a jump when Major emitted a piercing meow. Clem sat up, rubbing her eyes and tossing back her hair in a way that made her breasts jiggle most enticingly. As Josh reached for her, she laughingly struck his hand away. ''Major's hungry,'' she announced. ''We'd better get up and feed him.''

"After all, he's eating for four," said Josh. "And I am up."

She sneaked a look, blushed, and said overloudly, "My housecoat's on the floor on your side of the bed."

"You're no fun," Josh complained, leaning over to pick up the garment by his bed.

In a voice he had not heard her use before, Clem said, "You have a beautiful body, Josh."

The housecoat in his hand, the sheets swathed about his hips, Josh twisted to face her, the sun slanting across the dark hair on his chest, his belly taut. It was a very simple compliment; yet it left him temporarily speechless.

He pleased her. That was what she was saying.

Then she asked, tracing the roughened skin at the base of his rib cage, "What are those scars on your side?"

He handed her the housecoat and said awkwardly, "Oh, when the guerrillas found me with the bodies, there was a bit of a fracas...basically I went at them as if there were only two of them instead of a dozen. With entirely predictable results."

"You could have been killed," Clem whispered.

"At that point I'm not sure I cared."

"Then you would never have come here to my house and I wouldn't have met you again." A sheen of tears in her eyes, she played with the hem of the sheet. "I'm so glad you did come back, Josh. You see, ever since I was ten I've felt we had unfinished business, you and I—because I'd resented you so much I couldn't let you go, I was always aware at the back of my mind of carrying you with me." She glanced up. "When I saw your name on the letters of reference you gave me a month ago, and realized who you were, it was a terrible shock. No fun at all."

"But you don't feel that way now."

She gave him a sudden gamine smile. "We've certainly bridged the gap, haven't we?"

Clem was not telling him she loved him; but she certainly wasn't indifferent to him. Josh gathered her in a bear hug, said, "You'd better put your housecoat on or the cat's going to go hungry," and let her go.

She thrust her arms into the sleeves, swinging her long legs over the side of the bed and stretching with unselfconscious grace. Then she padded out of the room in her bare feet. Josh, feeling ten feet tall and as though he could take on twenty soldiers, pulled on his sweatpants and headed for the kitchen to see what he could make for brunch.

When Clem joined him there a few minutes later he was slicing mushrooms and peppers. He gave her a lazy smile. "Having impressed you with my amatory abilities, I shall now demonstrate that I'm no slouch in the kitchen, either. This will be my whatever-got-left-in-the-refrigerator-and-hasn't-yet-turned-green omelet."

"Risk was a word you used once, I believe?" she said, raising one brow.

A red pepper in one hand, the kitchen knife in the other, Josh said, "Are you really okay, Clem?"

Her gray eyes very clear, she replied, "I really am, Josh."

He put the things down, lifted her off the ground in an exuberant hug and whirled her around twice. "*I* feel fantastic!"

The omelet was a huge success, they left the dishes in the sink, and went out in the garden to do some raking. Because Josh was happy, the scarlet tulips seemed to shimmer in the sunshine and the singing of the birds pierced his ears with its beauty. The dry fusty scent of last year's leaves, the new sprigs of green grass were suffused with ultimate meaning; he whistled as he worked, occasionally bursting into song, and could not think of anywhere he would rather be than in this untidy old garden with Clem.

As she helped him layer the leaves in the compost pile, she said hesitantly, "I've never seen you so happy..."

"That's because I've never been so happy," he answered promptly.

She leaned on the rake, a faint perplexed frown between her brows. "All we did was make love, Josh."

He had been shoveling earth on top of the leaves. Staring at the rich brown clumps, he said, "For me, the earth moved."

"Yes. But——"

Suddenly afraid, because his happiness was so new and quite possibly fragile, he interrupted, "No big discussion, no high-powered emotion. Let's just accept it for what it was and be grateful."

"All right," she said, not looking totally convinced.

In a deliberate change of subject Josh said, "You've got some ashes from the fireplace we could add to this, haven't you?"

Clem accepted his lead; once they had finished with the compost, she edged some of the borders while he sawed some two-by-fours to prop up the fence. They made tea in Clem's kitchen, then she said, "I've got to have a shower, I'm mud to the elbows."

Josh leaned over and kissed her, a leisurely kiss to which she more than responded. "We could shower together," he said.

Color crept up her cheeks. "Another first."

"The omelet being the other one, I presume?"

"It was certainly a unique experience," she concurred.

Taking hold of her hand, Josh led her toward the bathroom. She went willingly, she helped undress him, she soaped his back and played with him both with the

innocence of a child and the burgeoning sensuality of a
woman newly awakened to the power of her femininity.
They then made love in her bed, a wild, tumultuous
lovemaking in which Josh unleashed some of the spon-
taneity that he had restrained the first time and Clem,
half shyly, half boldly, seized the initiative from him
more than once.

Finally satiated, they lay entwined under the covers.
Josh was almost asleep when Clem said artlessly, "I can't
imagine why I waited this long to make love—it's
wonderful!"

Through his happiness Josh felt a twinge of unease,
for she was speaking far too generally for his liking, and
the mere thought of her in bed with another man turned
unease to a most uncomfortable mixture of cold fear
and searing jealousy. Then, in the kitchen the telephone
rang, its shrill summons like an intruder, breaking in to
the intimacy of the bedroom, the peace of early evening.

Clem sat up. "That's probably Mother, she usually
calls on Sunday—I'd better answer it."

Josh turned on his back, hearing the low murmur of
her voice from the kitchen, wishing his unease would go
away. He was sure he was right to go slowly with Clem,
give her the time to get used this new intimacy before
telling her he loved her and wanted to marry her. One
thing at a time.

Marry her. He put his hands behind his head, gazing
up at the ceiling, which, he thought, could do with a
coat of paint. He was not sure when he had arrived at
the decision that Clem was the woman he wanted to
marry; he only knew the decision had been made. And
in his bones he knew it was the right decision.

One thing at a time, he told himself again. Don't rush
her.

A few minutes later Clem trailed back in the room. The shine had gone from her eyes. "That was Mother," she said. "She's coming for a visit."

"When?" Josh asked baldly.

"Just what I asked. But she hates being tied down to a specific time on a specific day—she'd rather be spontaneous." Clem gave a heavy sigh. "I don't think she'll come until next week, because she's getting some work done on her town house."

Josh's unease increased appreciably. Arabella affected Clem, even on the telephone long distance. What would it be like when she was here in the house? He hesitated. "Has she heard from my father, do you know?"

"I didn't ask."

Clem's face was set forbiddingly. Josh persisted, "But you told her I was living here in your house?"

"She'll find out when she gets here," said Clem.

Worse and worse. "Well," Josh said, "it'll be an interesting scene if I'm the one to open the door to her."

Clem's smile had a touch of malice. "Won't it?" Restlessly she opened the door to her wardrobe and began flipping through the hangers.

"Clem," Josh said, "come here."

"I'm busy."

Swiftly disentangling himself from the sheets, he leaped to the floor and pulled her around to face him. He said forcefully, "Stop worrying, everything'll be all right—I'm not going to disappear just because your mother appears on the scene, and I won't embarrass you while she's here by hauling you down on the carpet and making love to you." His grin was crooked. "Although I might want to."

"I change when she's around," Clem said tightly. "That's why I don't invite her here very often."

Feeling his way, Josh ventured, "If she's been on her own for four years, maybe she's changing too."

"Maybe."

But she did not sound convinced. Rubbing the tension from her shoulders, Josh said, "Why don't I take you out for dinner tonight? And you could try and tell me why you change."

"She was always the one to break up the marriage!" Clem burst out. "As soon as she settles with one man, a better one appears, and off Mother goes. She *wrote* the cliché that the grass is greener on the other side of the fence."

"So all four men were faithful to her?"

"Well, not exactly . . . my father and your father were, but Andy had an affair with his secretary and Eric didn't know how to be faithful—but it was always Mother who left."

"Have you ever yelled at her? Told her how you feel about all this?"

"Of course not," Clem said shortly. "She'd be terribly hurt."

"So instead you were prepared to remain an unmarried virgin your entire life."

She snapped, "You sure took care of the latter."

"With your full cooperation," Josh retorted, and forbore to say that he planned to take care of her marital status as well. "Are we having a fight, Clem?"

"That's what happens when I talk about my mother, I get bitchy and horrible."

"I'm not running for shelter, neither am I fainting by the bedside," Josh said dryly. "Do you like Chinese food?"

"Love it," she answered with a troubled smile. 'But——"

"I'll make a reservation and get dressed and come down for you in half an hour?"

She let her eyes wander down the naked length of his body. "I would certainly recommend you get dressed."

"If I don't, we'll be here for the rest of the day."

"You have a one-track mind, Joshua—there are other appetites to satisfy," Clem said firmly, her smile much more convincing. "And making love makes you hungry. Unromantic, but true."

They talked about everything except Arabella at the Chinese restaurant and went for a long walk afterward, during which Josh's unease was swallowed up in the same unreasoning happiness of the morning. When they climbed up the steps to the front porch, he said lightly, "Will you sleep in my bed tonight or shall I sleep in yours?"

Clem had been turning the key in the lock; her hand stilled and the look she gave him was almost hunted. "We're not moving in together," she said.

"I wasn't suggesting we do. Just spend the night together, that's all."

"Oh." She wriggled her shoulders, visibly trying to relax. "Well, you have a choice of Major, or Rosebud and Armand."

"Rosebud," Josh replied, from a deep need to imprint himself on her part of the house.

So they slept in Clem's room that night, made love in the middle of the night, a lovemaking as sensuous as a dream, and Josh drove her to work the next morning. He then started considering his tactics for creating a job for himself, for he now knew he wanted to stay in Halifax rather than rejoin the oil company in any of its bases around the world. He had already given some thought of setting himself up as a legal adviser for environmental groups. His mother had left him enough when she'd died that he did not need a large salary, and he had banked much of his pay from the oil company; he could afford to bide his time, research the possibilities thoroughly, and, he hoped, make a valid contribution.

He also phoned the police station and found out that Brad was being arraigned that morning, and phoned a country inn on the south shore to make a reservation for Friday night. Late in the afternoon he went to three flower shops, returned briefly to the house, then picked Clem up from work.

In deference to her fellow workers, Josh kissed her decorously on the cheek before driving off. But at the first red light Clem rested her hand on his on the wheel, gazing in fascination at their linked fingers. "I thought about you all day," she blurted out. "It was awful; I couldn't concentrate at all."

Feeling much as he had felt the first time they had made love, Josh leaned over and kissed her open mouth. The light changed and the driver behind him leaned on the horn. Clem jumped and put her hand back in her lap. In a clash of gears Josh crossed the intersection.

"How's Major?" Clem asked in a faint voice.

"He's—she's—fine. He moved the kittens from my blue sweater to the laundry basket in my closet. I took the sweater to the dry cleaners, but they didn't hold out much hope."

They talked very carefully on neutral subjects the rest of the way home. Josh unlocked the front door, his heart already thumping in his chest so loudly he was sure she would hear it. He closed the door behind them and said, "Come here, Clem."

She walked blindly into his arms and they kissed as voraciously as if they had been apart for a week rather than nine hours. Her handbag dropped to the floor; her coat followed it, and Josh felt her hands slide under his shirt, her fingers tugging at the hair on his chest. He clasped her hips, pulling her to him, murmuring her name between hot, hungry kisses. Then she was taking him by the hand, pulling him toward her room, and his blood thickened with love for her, his impetuous and passionate Clem.

At the doorway of the room she stopped dead, and he heard the tiny exhalation of her breath. "Josh," she whispered. "Oh, Josh..."

In the three flower shops he had visited that afternoon Josh had bought every red rose they owned, and had strewn them all over her bed; they glowed with rich and pagan color on the white spread. Clem turned toward him and he saw that she was crying, slow tears seeping from her eyes and running down her cheeks. "That's the most beautiful thing you could possibly have done," she choked.

He drew her into his embrace, wondering if he would ever be able to anticipate her responses. He had hoped she would be pleased; he had feared she might be angry at his presumption. But he had not expected tears. "I didn't mean to make you cry," he said.

"I'm not crying because I'm sad—it's because I'm overwhelmed...I just think I'm beginning to know you and then you take me completely by surprise."

This was so exactly the way he felt about her that Josh could think of nothing to say. She burrowed her face into his chest, adding with a weak giggle, "I'm not going to squash all those gorgeous roses by making love on top of them...anyway, there are probably thorns. We'll have to go upstairs."

So they did.

CHAPTER EIGHT

ON MONDAY night Clem slept in Josh's bed, although she did go downstairs and arrange the red roses in as many vases as she could find and place them all over the house. On Tuesday they slept in Clem's room, accompanied by Armand; Rosebud was clearly resentful of the amount of room that Josh took up in the bed and stationed herself on the window ledge instead, staring at him balefully. Josh was impervious to Rosebud's displeasure, for Josh was happy.

On Sunday his happiness had been new and correspondingly fragile; by now he was having trouble remembering what Saturday had been like. Clem loved being in bed with him; he knew that, for she demonstrated it with all the generosity and passion that had lain dormant in her for years. But although his happiness was so strongly rooted in the physical, it was also founded on the sure knowledge that he loved her, and that each time they came together she was revealing more of herself, and thereby revealing a growing trust in him.

Give her time. It had become his talisman, and it was working. He was right to wait. He was right to keep his love for her to himself for now. The time would come for him to share it with her, of that he was becoming increasingly sure...but not yet.

On Wednesday when he drove her to work in the morning, he said as usual, "Pick you up around five-fifteen?"

She hesitated, then said with attempted casualness, "No need to get me today. I've got a couple of errands to do, so I'll catch the bus. Douglas is coming for supper; he's finished exams but he's got a research paper to hand in that I promised I'd proofread for him." She reached for the door handle.

Feeling as though someone had just punched him in the pit of his stomach, Josh grabbed at her sleeve. "Hold it," he said. Although rationally he knew Douglas was no threat to him, that Douglas and Clem had never been anything but friends, his gut was giving him a very different message; his gut was screaming danger. He added, also striving to sound casual, "You could invite me to supper, as well. I'd leave you to the proofreading afterward."

Clem's arm under her sweater was tense, much too tense for a simple discussion of a shared meal. She said, gazing through the windshield as though the dirty pavement were the most fascinating sight she had ever seen, "If you came to supper Douglas would guess that we were lovers—I know he would, he's very astute."

"So what?"

She transferred her attention from the pavement to Josh. "I don't want him to know!"

"Ashamed of me, Clem?"

"Don't be ridiculous," she said shortly. "Of course not. But it's private, what we do... nothing to do with anyone else."

"We're going out with Sharon and Jamie on Saturday."

"They're so wrapped up in themselves they'll never notice."

Josh was not so sure about that. He said quietly, "I'd like the chance to get to know your friends, Clem, I know they're important to you."

She had that hunted look on her face again as she said with a defiance that infuriated him, "I have a date with Manuel tomorrow night."

"Cancel it."

"And what reason would I give him? Oh, sorry, Manuel, but I've just started sleeping with my tenant so I can't go out with you?"

Josh forced his anger down. He said evenly, "Tell him you've met someone who's important to you and so for a while you're only going to date one person."

"I've never done that—I've always dated more than one man at a time."

"Dammit, we're lovers, Clem! I take that seriously, even if you don't."

"Of course I do, I've never made love with anyone before and it's a whole new scene to me; I take it very seriously. But it doesn't mean the rest of my life goes on hold."

"So what does it mean?"

She twisted her arm. "You're hurting."

He relaxed his fingers, realizing that in his anger he had been holding her with unconscious strength. "Sorry... look, we shouldn't let this get out of hand." He swallowed hard, striving for patience, tolerance, understanding, all the virtues that seemed to vanish when he pictured Clem dating another man, and went on, "I can understand that you have some commitments you made before Sunday that you want to keep—the date with Manuel, for instance. I don't like it, but I'll put up with it." His voice roughened, "But I won't be the guy you sleep with when it's convenient for you and then the rest of the week you date whomever you please."

"Oh, won't you?" she snapped.

"No, I won't! If you and I are lovers, you won't be dating anyone else. And that includes Manuel. It's all or nothing, Clem. Because I'm not going to sit around every evening wondering——"

With evident relief Clem interrupted him. "There's Louise, I've got to go."

Josh kept hold of her wrist, anger and frustration still churning not far from the surface. "You're not getting out of it that easily—we'll continue this tonight when Douglas has gone." Then he put his other hand under her chin, ignoring her furious face to give her a long hard kiss. "You're going to have to stop running one of these days. Might as well be now as later."

Her cheeks were scarlet. "You don't own me!"

Very deliberately Josh ran his finger along the soft curve of her lip. "I'm the man who held your naked body in his arms all night... and I'm not going to go away. Think about it, Clem." Then, with an equally deliberate lightness, he gave her hair a little tug and said, "Have a nice day... and don't forget to hide the roses before Douglas arrives, will you?"

She shot him a scathing look, got out of the car, slammed the door and stalked across the pavement. Josh drove away.

He went home, put on his running gear and jogged for nearly four miles, trying to run off his anger. Because under the anger lay pain that Clem could treat him so cavalierly; that she would even want to date anyone else. The pain was of an intensity that frightened him: the dark side of love.

By the time he was stretching out his calf muscles against the side of the house he had exorcised most of his anger, and reason had usurped emotion. He had removed Clem's fear of sex, he had no doubt of that. What he was dealing with now was her fear of commitment. She had always sought safety in numbers, and now he

was asking her to change that pattern, to devote herself
to him alone.

It was her basic conflict, one he had hoped to avoid
for longer than three days.

*You could have kept your mouth shut about Douglas
and Manuel. You're the one who started the fight, not
Clem.*

Sure, he jeered back. And could I have stood in the
doorway waving goodbye while she dated every other
man in Halifax?

Jealous, Josh?

Damn right I am.

Which seemed to be the end of that particular dialog.
Josh went inside, showered, and headed for the library,
where he began listing the various environmental groups
in the province and their mandates. He ate both lunch
and dinner out, lifted weights at the gym and swam for
half an hour, and then at about ten o'clock drove back
to the house. Douglas's battered old car was parked on
the street.

Josh knew exactly what he was going to do.

He let himself in the front door, whistling "See, The
Conqu'ring Hero Comes." Then he called out Clem's
name, and without waiting for an answer walked into
her living room. Douglas was lying on the couch, nose
buried in a thick textbook. Clem, pencil in hand, had
been reading through a pile of manuscript. Josh said in
a friendly manner, "Hi, there, Douglas...I hear exams
are over, that must be a weight off your mind."

Then, turning to Clem and letting his voice deepen
with an emotion that was by no means false, he said,
"Hello, sweetheart, you look very studious."

Her mouth fell agape; Josh kissed it without haste
and with evident enjoyment and said, "Mind if I get

myself some juice, hon? I got carried away in the weight room."

The inferences were obvious: he was at home with her body, and he was at home in her kitchen. And neither Clem nor Douglas was at all slow-witted.

Fury, panic and a wayward gleam of laughter at his effrontery warred in Clem's gray eyes. Douglas was hidden from her by Josh's body; she pulled a hideous face at Josh and said sweetly, "Help yourself. By the way, someone called Xanthia phoned an hour ago. She seemed very disappointed that you weren't home."

Touché, thought Josh, with a flash of admiration. "I have absolutely nothing to say to Xanthia," he said coolly. "Want a coffee, love? Douglas, can I get you something to drink?"

Douglas was sitting up and had closed the textbook, whose spine announced it dealt with diseases of the pancreas. Running his fingers through his close-cropped reddish hair, his thin face alight with laughter, he said, "Clem, you're a dark horse—why didn't you tell me about you and Josh?"

"There's nothing to tell," Clem said coldly.

"Then why so many red roses in the spare room? It looks like a flower shop. Or a funeral parlor."

"Douglas, the door to the spare room was closed!"

"That's where you're wrong—I told you a while ago that most of the latches in this house need replacing. And ten dozen red roses aren't exactly inconspicuous; I noticed them when I went to the bathroom." He gave Josh a man-to-man grin. "Congratulations! Best news I've heard in a long time, I've always figured the right man for Clem would come along sooner or later... you realize there'll be a good many guys in Halifax who'll be wondering what you've got that they haven't?"

Each word falling like an ice crystal, Clem said, "I would appreciate it if you'd stop discussing me as if I didn't——"

"Come off it, Clem," Douglas chuckled. "You've been on the run for years, and I'm happy you've stopped, that's all. There's no rush for that paper; why don't you finish it in the next couple of days and I'll drop by and pick it up before the weekend?" He got up, stretching lazily. "I'll take a raincheck on the coffee, Josh…three's a crowd, and all that." Then he turned to Clem and for a moment his tired, pleasant face was very serious. "I'm genuinely happy for you, Clem. No good running—you only carry your burdens with you—I learned that a long time ago. And you're much too alive to be living like a nun." He kissed her on both cheeks and gave Josh a comradely grin. "I'll let myself out."

As the front door clicked shut Josh said, "He'll make an extremely good doctor. Say it, Clem, before you burst."

Clem, unexpectedly, burst into tears.

Aghast, Josh took her in his arms, smoothing her tangled curls, hearing her sob into his T-shirt, "You s-scare me to death. You run over me like a steamroller, I don't know where I am any more, everything's turned upside d-down…"

He waited until her sobs had diminished into snuffles, rubbing his cheek in her hair, which smelled of the herbal shampoo she used; her curls were springy, as full as energy as Clem herself. "I'm not going to apologize for what I did," he said. "And I'm not going to promise I won't do it again tomorrow night, either."

She raised a flushed, tear-streaked face. "Don't push too hard, Josh."

"I'll push as hard as I have to," he said inflexibly, his eyes boring into hers.

With the reckless courage he loved in her, Clem tilted her chin, disdaining to wipe one last tear that was trickling down her cheek to her chin. "A battle of wills," she said. "May the best person win."

"I'd much rather that we both win," Josh rejoined. "That's what I'm fighting for. If I lose you, I sure won't be a winner. And I'm conceited enough to figure you're better off with me than without me."

Her lashes flickered. "You have an answer for everything, don't you?" she said, tossing her head, her curls bouncing. "Do you have an answer for this?"

Pressing herself into him, rubbing her breasts against his chest in slow movements, she slid her arms around his neck and began kissing him, kisses of such blatant invitation that his heart began to pound in thick heavy strokes. She had caught his lower lip between her teeth; desire slammed through him, hot and urgent. Without finesse or gentleness, he picked her up and carried her through to her bedroom, where he stopped by the bed, kicking off his deck shoes.

Clem pulled him down on top of her, wrapping her thighs around him to hold him captive, kissing him with a wantonness that made his head reel. Her hands were everywhere on his body, beneath his thin shirt, fumbling with the buckle of his belt; without him being quite sure how it had happened, he found himself naked beside her on the bedspread. Only then did she start taking off her own clothes, garment by garment, teasing him with the slow unveiling of her body, her eyes glittering.

Wondering if he would ever know her or be able to anticipate what she would do next, his wild and wayward Clem, Josh allowed himself to be drawn deeper and deeper into the vortex of a passion as sharp as a knife-edge, as red as the heart of the rose. And his last coherent thought concerned his use of that word allow... was he allowing himself? Or did he indeed have any choice?

Josh woke the next morning in Clem's bed, to the hiss of spray from the shower; Clem was already up, Armand was curled into his knees, and Rosebud had taken possession of Clem's pillow. Her amber eyes regarded Josh coldly.

Although Josh had slept like the dead, he had the sensation that he had been dreaming the whole night, disconnected, disturbing dreams whose images eluded him yet whose mood remained with him. Stretching his legs, his brain leaping into instant action, he began to think.

He had achieved what he had wanted to achieve last night, despite Douglas's presence: he had spent the night in Clem's bed. Yet had their lovemaking been in any sense an expression of love? Or had it simply been an extension of the battle of wills, a power struggle, with anger underlying it rather than caring and affection?

It was not the fact that Clem had taken the initiative; he had loved her for that. It was why she had.

The shower had shut off and he heard the soft pad of her footsteps in the hall. He had no answers to any of his questions, and was only conscious of an inner sense of discord, of edginess, that he did not want to share with her. He buried his face in the pillow and closed his eyes.

Clem's movements as she dressed seemed to him stealthy, as though she was trying not to waken him. Then he heard her creep out of the room. She had gone to the kitchen, because the tap ran, the toaster clicked, the kettle boiled. A few minutes later he heard her clean her teeth. Then the front door closed behind her.

She had made no attempt to wake him, and she had not kissed him goodbye. He got up, made the bed as best he could without disturbing the two cats, and went for a run.

Josh had dinner that evening with the coordinator of all the environmental groups in the area, a charming sixty-year-old woman with flyaway gray hair that reminded him of Clem's and an attitude of unquenchable optimism tempered by realism that he found very attractive. She also promised him more work than he could handle, and challenges enough for two. They parted at nine-thirty, mutually pleased with each other.

When Josh got back to the house, Manuel's car, a sleek black sports car, was nowhere in sight. For a moment Josh sat in his own car, reluctant to go inside. The meeting with Charlotte Melby had occupied the larger part of his attention all evening; but the unease he had wakened with this morning was still with him, and as he gazed through the windshield at Clem's house it intensified. Manuel was not Douglas. Manuel was a handsome and successful stockbroker, an accomplished skier, an escort any woman would be proud to have.

He was no doubt as accomplished in bed as he was on the ski slopes. He had that look about him.

But Clem had known Manuel for over six months and had not slept with him. So why the hell was he worrying?

He was worrying because in the last few days Clem had lost her fear of sex. She might be all too ready to fall into Manuel's arms. The traditional ripe plum.

Come off it, Josh, this is Clem we're talking about. Clem's straight. She's the last woman to go from you to someone else all in twenty-four hours.

The mere thought of her touching Manuel, hugging him, kissing him—Josh's imagination could go no further than this—caused him to break out in a cold sweat, and made his maxim of giving her all the time she needed seem positively suicidal.

Give her time.

When she comes home tonight tell her you love her and want to marry her.

Josh pounded his fist on the wheel in frustration, wondering if love was always this difficult. How blithely he had assumed he would find the right woman and that she would be equally delighted to be found! Conceited fool, he castigated himself. You've found the right woman, all right. But how to convince her he was the right man was another matter.

He had tomorrow night. The country inn, the king-size bed—minus Rosebud—firelight and champagne.

He took a couple of deep breaths, trying to expel the tension in his muscles, and then got out of the car and went into the house. As he stepped in the front hall, shucking off his raincoat, Clem came out of her living room.

"You're home early," said Josh, light-headed with relief. She was not with Manuel. She was home.

In a clipped voice Clem said, "Manuel called me at work this afternoon; he has the flu. So we made a date for next week instead."

She had not been with Manuel after all; but she had not used the opportunity to break with Manuel.

She could have. Very easily.

With great care Josh pushed the loop on his coat over the hook, not trusting himself to speak or to look at her. Instead he found himself wishing with passionate intensity that he had never seen the rental advertisement, that he had never come to this house and renewed acquaintance with the woman standing not ten feet away from him.

Clem said, to his ears sounding merely defiant, "It's no big deal, Josh—you don't have to look like that."

If it's no big deal, why are you doing it? He felt a wave of exhaustion swamp him, the weakness in his knees and the racing of his heart both symptoms he had almost forgotten. He straightened his spine, because he refused to make a bid for her sympathy, and said, "Do what you have to do, Clem. Good night." Then he wheeled and headed for the stairs.

"I don't know why you're making such a fuss," she cried. "It's not as though I'd ever sleep with him."

Josh was suddenly filled with an ice-cold rage. "Grow up!" he retorted. "Teenagers have a different date every night of the week . . . twenty-eight-year-old women know the meaning of commitment. I don't make love to you because we happen to live in the same house—I make love to you because you're special to me and I care about you."

"I never asked you to care!"

He looked at her almost with hatred. "I won't be used, in bed or out—do you hear?"

Clem said frigidly, "The way you're shouting, I should think Manuel can hear."

Josh drew a deep breath, trying to subdue the red mist of rage before his eyes. "You know, it's ironic—men are the ones who are always accused of detaching their feelings when they make love . . . but if you can't handle my feelings, Clem, we're better off sleeping in different beds. Which is what we're going to do tonight and what we'll continue to do until you figure out what you want."

Fueled by anger, he took the stairs two at a time, went into his bedroom and closed the door. He then sat down hard on the bed, letting his head fall between his knees until the dizziness had passed.

It was Victorian maidens who were supposed to have fainting spells and go into declines, he thought bitterly. Not grown men.

That he had not had a single attack like this in over two weeks, he chose to ignore. Just as he tried to ignore the soreness of his heart that Clem would continue dating Manuel. He went to bed, read for a while without taking in the sense of what he was reading, fell asleep and woke up at three in the morning reaching for Clem.

Clem was not there. She was in a bedroom downstairs only a few yards away from him; yet she was so far from him that she might just as well have been on another continent.

At six o'clock Josh gave up any pretense that he was sleeping, dressed in his rain gear and went out for a run. The fog had moved in from the Atlantic, cooling his face and clinging in tiny drops to his nylon shell. The buildings were blurred into insubstantial shadows, his fellow joggers into ghosts. And as he ran, the black thoughts that three in the morning had engendered ran with him. He loved Clem. He wanted to go away with her tonight. But under the circumstances he was almost sure he couldn't do it.

At seven he let himself back into the house, hauling his shell over his head. Through the wet yellow folds of nylon he heard Clem say in a small voice, "Couldn't you sleep either?"

Josh pulled his wrists free, his sweat-dampened T-shirt clinging to his heaving chest, and, to conceal the jolt that her presence always caused him, gave her a comprehensive survey from head to toe. "Clem," he said non-committally, "you really need a new housecoat."

Her old blue housecoat was belted around her waist and there were blue shadows under her eyes. "Are we still going away tonight?" she asked.

He knew her too well to suspect her of any mercenary motives. "Do you still want to?"

She nodded, her fingers restlessly pleating the pocket of her housecoat, her eyes avoiding his. He remembered how angry he had been with her the night before; he remembered the flickering glow of candlelight on her naked breasts two nights ago; he remembered the defiant girl of ten who had refused to cry when he had told her that her mother was having an affair with his father; and his heart turned over with love for her and his brain told him to give her all the time that she needed. Then he heard himself say, "But what about Manuel?"

She wrung her hands together with unconscious pathos. "You've got to give me time!"

Give me time. Inadvertently Clem had used the words to which he was most vulnerable. He might be all kinds of a fool; he might be digging his own grave. But how could he refuse her when she asked for the very thing he had been trying so hard to give her? "If you'd like to go, then we will," Josh said.

"That's more than I deserve."

"Yeah," he said.

She managed a smile, the shadows lifting a little from her face. "I'm looking forward to it, Josh..."

Already wondering if he'd done the right thing, Josh nodded. "I'll pick you up sharp at five."

She gave him a level look. "Once you've kissed me good morning, I'll get ready for work."

Clem was not stupid; Clem had heard the reservations in his voice. "If you're going to kiss me, you'd better hold your nose," he said. "I reached five miles this morning."

When she walked into the circle of his arms, the softness of her breasts and the generosity of her kiss worked their usual magic; his arousal was instant and noticeable. In between kisses he murmured, "You're quite a woman—five miles and look what you're doing to me."

Clem drew back, confusion written all over her features. "When I'm with you everything is so simple! We feel absolutely right together. It's only when I'm away from you that I start feeling frightened and trapped."

Josh said forcefully, "You're still living your mother's life, Clem—you've got to learn to live your own. Because you're not her."

She pulled free. "That's just slick psychology."

"It's reality."

"Please, Josh, no more fights," she pleaded.

"You think about it." Trying to lighten his tone, he added, "Go take your shower—and don't take all the hot water."

Three-quarters of an hour later he drove her to work.

CHAPTER NINE

JOSH came back to the house, and by midmorning was deeply immersed in the pile of literature Charlotte Melby had given him. He was finding the creating of his own job exciting; he'd get Pete to recommend an accountant to him for the financial end of things.

He was immersed in the intricacies of a court case against a forestry company that had been spraying private land with herbicides when he heard a car door slam outside and then, a few moments later, footsteps mounting the stairs. He waited for the doorbell to ring, and instead heard the front door open and then the sound of voices, a man's and a woman's.

Josh pushed back his chair and glanced out of the window; a taxi was parked outside. Was Clem ill? But surely she would have called him, rather than a cab. Frowning, he left the room and started down the stairs, and as he did so the front door opened.

The woman standing in the hall beside three glossy leather suitcases gave a tiny shriek of alarm when she heard his approach. Then she tilted her chin in a way he immediately recognized. "Who are you?" she demanded.

She had a head of artfully and expensively arranged black curls and big blue eyes, and although she was well into middle age she carried herself with the pride of a woman who in her youth had been extremely beautiful. She was still beautiful; but not as beautiful as he remembered.

He said slowly, descending the last few stairs, "Don't you know who I am?"

She fidgeted with the collar of her elegant linen suit, the diamonds on her fingers sparkling with cold fire. She and Josh were standing level with each other now, and the sun that had broken through the fog slanted across his face. Under her flawless makeup the color drained from her features. In a shocked whisper she said, "You're Joshua—Graham's son!"

"And you're Arabella."

"What are you doing here? Where's Clem?"

"I——"

Arabella took three steps toward him, looking very fierce. "What have you done with her?"

"She's at work," Josh said loudly. "What did you think I'd do with her?"

"Are you living with her?"

"No!"

Arabella looked disbelieving. "When she was nine, she thought the sun rose and set on you. If you're not living with her, what are you doing here?"

"You're a very direct lady, Arabella Delaney," Josh said dryly, liking the way she had sprung to the defense of her only child. "Clem unfortunately no longer thinks the sun rises and sets with me, and I'm renting the upstairs of her house, not living with her." He was not being strictly truthful here, but neither was he ready to be.

"Unfortunately?" she pounced.

He said smoothly, "Have you flown from Toronto this morning? You must be tired—let me put your cases in the spare room and make some coffee...we've got several years to catch up on, haven't we?"

Arabella's eyes, which were the youthful blue of forget-me-nots, regarded Josh with an astuteness that was new.

"You've grown into a very handsome man, Joshua ... more than handsome, because there's power there, and some hard experiences, I'd say. And do remember that the last time I saw you, you had maroon hair."

He grinned. "I'm glad you think I've improved."

"Don't fish for compliments. Are you telling me you're in love with Clem?"

"Coffee, Arabella ... you don't mind if I call you Arabella, do you?"

"I'm thinking of changing back to my maiden name," she said unexpectedly. "I don't feel like Mrs. Delaney anymore. Or Mrs. anyone else for that matter. So Arabella is fine. And coffee would be most welcome; it never ceases to astound me that a plane that can lift off the ground with two hundred passengers and all their luggage cannot produce a decent cup of coffee."

The Arabella Josh had known had needed the status of a man's name along with all the social implications of marriage; but that, he realized, was many years ago and she too had had some hard experiences. More and more interested in her, he picked up her cases and led her to the spare room, in which he was glad to see that only two vases of roses remained. "I'll put the coffee-pot on," he said and escaped to the kitchen.

She joined him in a few minutes, allowing him to pull out her chair and sat down, her back very straight. Josh, having decided to go on the offensive, said blandly, "What's the latest word from my father?"

A tiny muscle moved in Arabella's jaw. "He didn't tell me you were living in my daughter's house," she said roundly. "Neither did Clem. *Are* you in love with her?"

"Are you going to see my father?"

"Two equally unanswerable questions, is that what you're saying?" As Josh poured milk into a jug and put it on the table, she added with the directness he had already noticed, "We're old enemies, you and I."

"We were enemies fifteen or sixteen years ago. I don't want to be your enemy now, Arabella."

"It seems a waste of energy, doesn't it?" She sighed, looking every year of her age. "Your father was a good man, and deserved better than I... for all that I was in my thirties, I was very young then, and very silly."

"He wants to see you again, I know that."

Her long polished nails tapped on the table in a jerky rhythm. "I was beautiful once, Joshua. Now I'm over fifty and the best you can say about me is that I'm endeavoring to grow old gracefully. Gracefully—what a ridiculous word under the circumstances!"

"You look wonderful to me," Josh said sincerely.

"Men have this deplorable tendency to remember you as you were all those years ago," Arabella said. "Do you think I want to see the look in Graham's eyes when he sees the ravages of the last fifteen years? No, thank you!"

She was afraid; with genuine compassion Josh said, "My father's sixty-two, Arabella—he's not looking for a thirty-year-old. It's you he wants to see. The real you."

"I can't do it," she said raggedly. "I hate growing old. He asked me to send a photograph, and I won't even do that."

"Clem's as scared of marriage as you are of growing old," Josh said caustically. "You make a good pair."

"So did she turn you down?"

"I haven't asked her yet." He poured two mugs of coffee and sat down across from Arabella, thinking what an unlikely conversation this was to be having with a woman he had once hated with all the intensity of an adolescent.

"Do you love her?"

"Yes."

She gave him a keen glance, perhaps not having expected so straightforward a response. "You and she are old enemies, too. After you told her what was going on between Graham and me, she hated you as passionately as she'd worshiped you."

"That's not the problem, Arabella." He hesitated. "I don't know any gentle way to say this—Clem, with the example of your four marriages before her, wants nothing to do with marriage. She won't even commit herself to dating one person, for God's sake!"

He heard the pain raw in his voice and cursed himself for exposing it. Arabella said sharply, "I've always loved her."

"That's not the issue. Clem grew up with change. So she's bought a house where she's determined to stay for the rest of her life, and she dates as many different men as she can so that none of them can tie her down. Which includes me."

"And which you hate."

"Damn right I do."

Arabella busily stirred cream in her coffee. "I've changed," she said in a small voice. "I've been alone now for four years, and, although I hated it at first and thought I'd die of loneliness, it's not so bad now that I'm used to it... I wouldn't want Clem to be alone all her life, though." She took a sip of coffee and added, looking pleasantly surprised, "A man who can brew a good cup of coffee—Clem ought to marry you. And you know, Joshua, part of growing old gracefully is taking an interest in grandchildren."

She was glancing at him through lashes every bit as long as Clem's. "My father has evinced an interest in future generations, too," Josh said, and watched the lashes drop to hide her eyes. "My father, I am sure, would find you not only graceful, but mature and interesting as well."

"He's not going to get the chance," Arabella announced, agitated. "What time does Clem get home from work? I might go shopping downtown, and meet her for lunch."

Josh was to have met Clem sharp at five so they could have dinner at the country inn. Schooling his face to hide his feelings, he said, "She usually goes for lunch at noon and she gets off at five or a little after."

"I'd like to take the two of you out for dinner," Arabella added. "Would that be possible?"

"Yes," said Josh, "that would be fine."

Half an hour later she left in a cab, having refused Josh's offer of a drive. Josh went upstairs and phoned the daycare center. Clem answered. "Clem? Josh. Your mother's on her way down to take you out for lunch."

Her voice sounded a long way away. "*Mother?* She's here?"

"Very much so. She also wants to take the two of us out for dinner tonight."

"I didn't think she'd come this soon..."

Josh said roughly, "I'll have to cancel our reservation."

"Oh, heavens, I'd forgotten about that. Of course you will."

Wishing he could see her face, for she sounded a million miles away and there was almost no emotion in her voice, he demanded, "How long does she usually stay?"

"A week to ten days."

He said exactly what was on his mind. "We won't be able to make love the whole time she's here."

She made an indeterminate sound. "I guess not."

"Clem, don't you *care*?"

"You knew she was coming for a visit, Josh."

"I'd hoped we'd have tonight together."

"Well, we can't. I can't talk about it now, Christine is at the dentist so we're really busy...I'll see you tonight."

Josh was left holding the receiver, which was reverberating with an empty hum. He slammed it into its cradle, swore in a colorful mixture of English and Arabic, and rang the country inn to cancel the reservation. He then checked his watch. Eleven-thirty. Seven-thirty in British Columbia. Graham had always been an early riser. Not stopping to think, he dialed the eleven numbers and waited while the connections clicked into place across four thousand miles.

On the third ring Graham picked up the phone. "Hello?"

"Dad, it's Josh. Have you got plans for tomorrow night?"

"Nothing I can't get out of. Why?"

"Arabella arrived here this morning."

After several seconds of expensive silence Graham asked, "Did she say she wanted to see me?"

"Well, not exactly. But Clem and I have been invited out for dinner tomorrow night and Arabella will probably go with us—she might prefer to have an escort."

"She doesn't know you're phoning me."

"No."

"I keep getting double messages from her...she always seems pleased to hear from me, but when I suggest we get together she stalls."

Although Josh knew why, he couldn't very well say so. "You could use the excuse that you came to see me."

"And insult her intelligence? I'll book a flight today if I can get one, and call you back . . . maybe you could check on a hotel for me. How are you and Clem getting along?"

"Don't hold your breath for those grandchildren," Josh said, and changed the subject to the most suitable hotel.

Fifteen minutes later Graham called back with flight times, and Josh gave him the name of the hotel. Then, wondering if he would get in trouble for so blatantly playing God, Josh went out jogging.

Late Saturday morning, at Arabella's insistence, Josh joined the two women for coffee in the garden. A pair of chickadees was nesting in the maple by the fence, and in the far corner a fat robin was having an energetic wash in the bird bath. The primroses were in bloom, and the quince was a blaze of orange; Clem discussed these things one by one in the same brittle voice she had used all last evening, a voice that seemed to reduce Arabella to silence. Arabella, Josh was quite sure, had not told Clem about her loneliness or her fears.

He did not like this new Clem; she was as different from the woman of passion and generosity who had shared his bed as she could be. Into one of the silences that had a tendency to fall like stones into their conversation, he said, "By the way, my father's in town...he phoned me half an hour ago. I suggested he join us for dinner this evening."

Both women were staring at him, Arabella with terror, Clem with outright suspicion. Arabella gasped, "Does he know I'm here?"

"He's looking forward to seeing you again," Josh said with careful truth.

Clem said rudely, "You set this up, Josh."

At last there was some feeling in her voice. He said, "That's the first time you've looked me in the eye since we sat down."

She was not only meeting his eye: she looked as if homicide was high on her list. Arabella said faintly, "I'll have to do my nails... and what will I wear? Darling, would you come downtown with me this afternoon? I saw a dress I liked yesterday and you could tell me if you think it would be suitable."

"Mother, you were married to Graham for two years— you don't have to make such a fuss."

With undoubted dignity Arabella said, "I should never have left him... that was the biggest mistake of my life. Of all the men I've been married to, he was the kindest."

Through gritted teeth Clem said, "So are you thinking of marrying him again?"

Arabella put down her coffee cup, her hand shaking very slightly. "Clem, I'm sorry I got married four times, and I'm sorry your life was so unsettled. But I am trying to learn from my mistakes, and that's all anyone can do."

"I apologize, Mother," Clem said in that same brittle voice, "I shouldn't have said that. It's none of my business what you do."

A tiny yellow-feathered warbler landed on the lilac bush beside them. Clem pointed it out with great relief and the conversation gathered momentum again. Half an hour later Arabella went inside to get ready for the shopping expedition; Clem put the cups on the tray and said nastily, "You're really into playing God, aren't you?"

Josh stood up. "It occurred to me that I might be doing that. But I thought it was worth the risk."

She banged the jug onto the tray so hard that milk slopped to the rim. "She'll only be hurt again!"

"My father's never stopped loving her, Clem."

"You had no right to bring the two of them together in my house."

Before she could pick up the tray, Josh grasped her by the shoulders, pushing her into the dappled shadow of the lilac trees. "You're being very unfair to her," he said vehemently. "Yes, she was a shallow and selfish woman who totally disrupted your life and I can see why you'd be angry with her. But she's been on her own for four years now and she's had lots of time to think. You're still seeing her as the woman she was—you're blind to how she's changed."

"If she marries your father, you and I will be tied together for the rest of our lives!"

She was wearing a thin cotton top, through which he could feel the warmth and softness of her skin. He said hoarsely, "We're tied together anyway," and kissed her on the mouth.

She resisted him furiously, shoving against his chest; he moved his hands to her waist and without subtlety hauled her against the length of his body. Then with one hand he found the swell of her breast, and, as suddenly as it had arisen, his anger died. "I want you so much," he whispered, leaving a trail of kisses along the line of her jaw. "If your mother stays ten days, I think I'll go out of my mind."

All the fight went out of her; she buried her fingers in his hair, pulled his head down and kissed him so explicitly that he wondered dimly if he was going out of his mind already. When they finally pulled apart, the mingled sound of their breathing was harsh in the air and in the stormy gray of Clem's eyes he saw his own passion reflected. "Oh, Josh..." she said helplessly. "How long is it since you moved in...just over a month? I don't know where I am any more! I thought I had life all nicely figured out and I was content with my house and my friends, and now everything's shifted and tumbled down around me just as if there'd been an earthquake."

She looked bewildered and unhappy; Josh hardened his heart and said, "Cows are contented."

"You don't give any quarter, do you?" she flashed.

"Not where it's not needed. Sure, I could have done without your mother landing on us right now. But you've got to deal with her sooner or later, Clem, and it might as well be now as next week or next month." His smile was crooked. "She wants grandchildren, too."

"Too?"

"So does my father." Before she could say anything, he ran his finger down the side of her face, his blue eyes very serious. "Would you like to have a child, Clem? My child?"

Her whole body went still. In a choked voice she said, "That's a crazy question!"

"Considering the way we've been behaving since last Sunday, I don't think it's so crazy."

Clem said helplessly, "It's a question I can't possibly answer...will you bring the tray?" She ducked under the fragrant branches of the lilac and dashed for the house.

She had not said no. But neither had she said yes. Josh picked up the tray and followed her.

At quarter to six Josh went to the hotel to pick up his father. Graham was waiting in the lobby, looking trim and fit in a new suit, and clutching a large bouquet of roses that Josh was glad to see were yellow, not red. The two men hugged each other, Graham protecting the roses; then Graham said, "How do I look?"

Josh stood back. "Great. Arabella's nervous too, Dad."

"She can't be as nervous as I am—I feel like a kid on his first date. How do you know she's nervous?"

"She bought a new dress and changed the color of her nail polish twice," Josh said promptly.

"New suit, new tie, and when I had a last-minute shave half an hour ago I dropped my razor and smashed it," Graham responded with a ghost of a smile. "Sounds like a draw." He squared his shoulders with the air of a man going to his execution. "Let's go."

Josh drove to Clem's and followed Graham up the front steps; Clem came out of the living room as they entered the house. She was wearing the ten-dollar black dress, her hair fastened high on her head, and Josh's heart did its familiar swoop in his chest at the sight of her. But she was not looking at him. She held out her hand, her smile rather fixed. "Hello, Graham," she said.

Graham passed Josh the bouquet, took her hands in his, and kissed her on both cheeks, saying with unforced warmth, "Hello, Clem, how nice to see you again after all these years."

Clem relaxed perceptibly. Then Arabella walked out of the living room, dressed in blue silk, her spine ramrod-straight. "Good evening, Graham," she said and stuck out her hand as though he were a very fierce dog who might bite it off.

"Arabella...I'd have known you anywhere," Graham said quietly, clasping her hand in his and raising it to his lips.

And Arabella, plainly overwrought, blurted, "You're just saying that to be polite—I'm a middle-aged woman."

With his free hand Graham very gently traced the line of her jaw, where the flesh was no longer as firm as it had been. "We've each of us aged," he said. "But that's natural enough... and you're still the most beautiful woman I've ever seen."

There could be no mistaking his sincerity. Arabella's eyes filled with tears. "Thank you," she quavered. "I'm so happy to see you, Graham."

Josh cleared his throat. "You're forgetting these, Dad," he said, holding out the flowers.

Graham passed them to Arabella. "I haven't forgotten your favourite color," he said.

A tear plopped on the cellophane wrapping as Arabella took the bouquet and buried her nose in the yellow petals. Clem muttered, "We're a bit short on vases, but I'll find one for you, Mother," and fled to the kitchen. Josh made a commonplace remark about the rosebushes in Clem's garden, and with a twinge of amusement wondered if Graham would propose that very night. If only Clem could be equally amused.

But Clem in no way cast a damper on the evening; she talked, she laughed, she reminisced about the past and did her best to set Graham and Arabella at their ease. Only Josh, who knew her well, noticed that she drank rather a lot of wine and that there were tiny tension lines between her brows. Although he was proud of the way she was behaving, because he knew how deeply her conflicts were rooted, he also felt a long way away from her. Sharon and Jamie radiated happiness; Arabella and Graham had a tendency to gaze into each other's eyes in a way he found very touching; but Clem was seated at the far end of the table from him and her febrile gaiety kept him safely at a distance. If only he and she could go home and go to bed together, everything would be all right, he thought savagely. But they couldn't.

He did not even have the chance to speak to her alone that night. The next day, as it was Clem's day off, it had been arranged that they go for a drive along the south shore. They had lunch at—and Josh certainly saw the irony in this—a country inn, and then wandered the length of one of the beaches beyond Lunenburg, a beach almost deserted and spectacularly beautiful with its sweep of dunes and long curling breakers. It was also, Josh remembered, a beach the four of them had visited shortly before Graham's and Arabella's marriage.

Arabella had taken off her pretty slingback sandals and was wandering along the edge of the surf, the breeze playing with her full skirt; she looked very happy and not at all middle-aged. Graham, at her side, carrying her sandals, looked equally happy. Josh said to Clem, "We've been here before, remember?"

She said in a staccato voice, "I certainly do. A month to the wedding, a ridiculous attempt to pretend we were a normal happy family—how I hated you that day!"

With a nod Josh indicated the pair in front of them. "They're not thinking of the past. Relax, Clem."

"How can I?" she said in a furious undertone. "I've seen all this before and I know exactly what's going to happen. She'll marry him, and it's off we go again, one more turn on the merry-go-round."

"Give her credit for having changed, that's all you have to do," Josh retorted.

A wave surged up the sand toward Clem's sandaled feet. She leaped out of the way and hurried to catch up with the couple ahead of them. Infuriated by her stubbornness, Josh lagged behind. He had the feeling Graham had chosen this particular beach to heal something between him and Arabella; if only that healing could extend to Arabella's daughter.

The next day Graham and Arabella were to leave after lunch in a rented car. While Arabella was putting some final touches to her makeup, Graham said sedately, "Don't wait up for us, Josh, we'll probably be late."

"Fine," Josh responded without a trace of a smile. But inwardly he was exultant. Clem had mentioned yesterday she'd be home this evening; they would have several hours together.

He had three appointments that day, two with consultancy firms, the other with an accountant, all three equally interesting. However, the accountant was running late, so it was five-thirty when Josh turned up outside the daycare center. The door was closed and the lights were out. Clem must have caught the bus.

Deciding that the house was suffering from a plethora of roses, he stopped at a bakery and bought two pieces of her favorite chocolate cake before going home. But Clem was not one of the passengers getting off the bus at the end of the street, nor was she anywhere in the house. Josh hung up his business suit, showered and dressed in cords and an open-necked shirt, then went downstairs and put on the kettle.

By seven o'clock he was both hungry and angry. It was clear Clem was not coming home for supper. Had Manuel phoned? Or Stewart? Or Paul? Did it really matter which one? She had not come home: that was what counted. On an evening when she had known she and Josh would be alone in the house, she had chosen not to come home.

He ordered a pizza, ate more than was good for him, and drank two beers. The end results were indigestion and the realization that under his anger lay, twinned, hurt and jealousy. But below them, newly discovered, was another emotion, one that genuinely frightened him. Hopelessness. What was the good of pursuing Clem?

She had consistently refused to limit herself to one man, she had made a date with Manuel for Thursday night, and now she was gone again. He, Josh, was a fool to think she would change the pattern of her life for his sake. She had no intention of doing so.

Thoroughly depressed, Josh had a third beer. He prowled around the house, unable to settle down. Dusk settled over the garden and the street lights came on.

Who was she with? Why could she not see how Arabella had changed? And why did he care so much that he felt as though a snake were gnawing at his vitals, destroying him from within?

But as he sat in his darkened living room, unable to focus his attention on anything, his turmoil of emotion gradually coalesced into anxiety, an anxiety so acute as to banish all his other feelings. Belatedly he began to use his brain.

Clem had said she would be home this evening. Clem, for all her faults, was not dishonest. Therefore something must have happened.

Brad was out on bail.

CHAPTER TEN

THE hair stood up on the back of Josh's neck and he pushed himself up from the chair. While he'd been sitting here in a stew of jealousy and self-pity, Clem could be in danger. Hurt. Raped...his mind winced from the word.

He went into her kitchen, took the spare set of keys from the hook and left the house on the run. In eight and a half minutes he was parking outside the daycare center. Intuition had brought him here; logic told him it was the place to start. If she was not here, he would go to the police station and find out Brad's whereabouts.

The front door, which should have been locked, was not. As the knob turned easily in his hand, every nerve in Josh's body tightened. He closed the door behind him and listened, and the silence of a deserted house rang in his ears.

He snapped the lock, switched on the lights and walked down the hall, turning on lights as he went. Toys, brightly painted furniture, pictures on the walls, everything as it should be.

Upstairs he found only the same succession of empty rooms. Back down the stairs and into the kitchen. He was gazing at the gleaming countertops when he heard from below his feet a faint, low moan.

His pulse racing, Josh pulled a butcher's knife from the rack set high on the wall and opened the door to the basement. When he flipped the light switch, a single bulb came on, casting deep shadows in the corners. "Clem?" he called.

A shuffling sound came from the far corners, like rats. The prison flashed into his mind, and with every ounce of his willpower Josh forced it back and began descending the stairs. They creaked. If Brad was down there, he would certainly know Josh was on the way.

At the bottom of the stairs, met only by the fusty smell of an old cellar, Josh called Clem's name again.

Her voice was horribly weak. "I'm in here..."

Wishing he had a flashlight, he ducked beneath the heating vents and went around the furnace, a furnace as venerable as Clem's. The blackness pressed in on him, just as it had in her basement, except that this time he couldn't back down. Feeling his palms wet with sweat, despising the frantic pounding of his heart, and by now almost sure that if Brad had been here he was long gone, Josh found himself face-to-face with two doors, old wooden doors, unpainted.

Standing well back, he pushed the first door open. It was a storage room with a small window above eye level, the light from the street showing boxes on shelves, dusty bicycles and cobwebs. He pushed against the second door and met resistance.

"Boxes..." Clem said faintly. "Can't move them."

Josh put down the knife and tested the door with his foot, discovering that the resistance was at the base, and with all his strength pushed against it. The door inched inward. Gritting his teeth, he pushed harder.

With a thud something fell to the ground and suddenly he was in. Clem was on the floor amid a tumble of boxes, half propped up, and in the dim light from the bulb by the furnace Josh could see dirt streaking her face and clothes. He knelt by her, forgetting that he was in a small, dark space, and demanded, "Are you hurt? Was it Brad?"

"Brad?" she faltered. "No..."

His eyes adjusted to the gloom, he saw an ugly bruise on her forehead, and brushed it with his finger. She flinched away. "Stupid accident," she whispered. "Storing some stuff we'd ordered and the boxes fell on me...couldn't open the door and everyone else had gone."

He heaved the boxes to one side, stacking them against the shelves, then put his arms around her and helped her to her feet. She swayed against him, and with a little giggle said, "I'm like one of Major's kittens—can't stand up."

"And if I pick you up we'll both be decapitated by the furnace vents...here, hold on."

With some difficulty and much giggling from Clem, they navigated the vents and the stairs. Josh deposited her carefully in an adult-size chair in the hall, collected the knife and put it back, and switched off all the lights. Then he carried Clem out to his car. A couple of passing pedestrians gave them curious glances; no one else paid them any attention. Josh next, despite her protests, drove Clem to the emergency department of the nearest hospital, where within the hour she was checked over and sent home to rest.

It was now half-past eleven. Not to Josh's surprise, Graham's car was parked on the street. "They're home," he said unnecessarily.

Clem, who was still pale and shaken, murmured, "Oh, dear...explanations. Josh, I'm sorry I made you go into yet another dark basement."

With some surprise he said, "I really didn't mind it too much—too worried about you. I figured Brad had got to you, that's why I was brandishing the kitchen knife."

"I never asked what made you go to the daycare?"

"After I'd spent several hours cursing you up and down for dating someone else I remembered you'd said you'd be home, and got really worried. The daycare seemed the place to start."

"I'm glad you did—I wasn't looking forward to spending the night there." She shuddered. "Spiders."

He said evenly, "Are you still planning to see Manuel on Thursday?"

"Yes. And I don't have the energy to fight about that now."

Josh had no intention of starting a fight; feeling very tired, he got out of the car and helped her to the front door, where she was seized upon by Arabella and there was indeed a flurry of explanations. Half an hour later, when Graham was gone, Josh went up to bed.

Clem had told him the truth; she had planned to be home this evening and had only been prevented by an accident. But that did not alter the fact that she did date other men and intended to continue doing so. Which left him to deal with that peculiarly nasty combination of anger, hurt and jealousy.

Clem stayed home from work the next day, cosseted by Arabella and Graham. Josh spent most of the day in the law library, brushing up on environmental cases and trying to ignore a dull pain in his chest that had nothing to do with pizza and beer.

On Wednesday Clem went back to work and Josh spent the morning with the president of a conservation advocacy group; when he came home for lunch in a drenching rain shower, he found Graham and Arabella sitting at the kitchen table holding hands. Arabella looked radiant and Graham ten years younger. Josh said quizzically, "What's up?"

"We're getting married," said Graham.

"This time we'll do better," Arabella said, her blue eyes sparkling. "I know what I want now—I didn't fifteen years ago."

Josh kissed Arabella and hugged his father. "I'm really happy for you," he said warmly. "Do I get invited to the wedding?"

"Of course you do, and Clem, too," Graham said.

A faint shadow crossed Arabella's face. "I'm afraid she won't be as happy about it as you are, Josh."

"Give her time," Josh said, and inwardly wondered how much more time he was willing to give her.

"No signs of you two getting hitched?" Graham said, raising his brow.

Josh turned away, searching for a new box of tea bags in the cupboard. "Don't think that's going to work out," he said, keeping his back to them. "Orange pekoe or Earl Grey?"

"But you love her!" Arabella exclaimed with some of her daughter's impetuosity.

"Earl Grey," Graham said, making shushing motions at his future bride.

Josh shifted his shoulders, wishing this conversation had never started. "It takes two to tango, Arabella," he said. "Clem doesn't want to."

"I feel as though that's my fault," Arabella wailed. "If I talk to her, maybe I can help..."

"Maybe you'd better let the two of them sort it out themselves," Graham said firmly.

Arabella gave him a doubtful look. "I want everybody else to be as happy as we are," she said.

"You can't legislate that, Arabella, nice though it would be," Graham said. "We made extra sandwiches, Josh; they're in the refrigerator. How did your meeting go this morning?"

Grateful to his father for rescuing him, Josh got out the sandwiches and described the way his job was shaping up. After lunch he went back to the library, and purposefully did not go home until nearly six, to allow Graham and Arabella time to share their news with Clem. But when he came in the door he heard Graham's voice from the living room. "...getting married. We're very happy, Clem, and we hope our news will make you happy, too."

There was the smallest of pauses. Then Clem said, a fraction too loudly, "Congratulations! Mother... Graham, my best to you both."

"You don't mind?" Arabella asked, sounding very nervous.

"Of course not! How could I? After all, I'm not ten years old now, Mother."

She was doing a good job, thought Josh, and was pleased that she was trying hard not to hurt either her mother or his father. But she was not telling the truth. She did mind; he knew she did.

Arabella apparently accepted her words at face value. "Oh, I am glad, dear," she said. "I know this is my fifth marriage——"

"Fifth and final," Graham declared.

"Well, exactly," Arabella said. "But I was afraid you might not like the idea, Clem."

"Of course I do."

"Wonderful!" Arabella burbled. "And who knows, maybe you'll soon be making Josh just as happy as we are, darling."

Josh winced and took an involuntary step forward. Graham said, "Arabella——"

"I know I promised I wouldn't mention it, Graham, but all I want is for Josh and Clem to be together too, keeping it all in the family, as it were."

"I'm not sure I know what you're talking about," Clem said carefully.

Josh took another step forward, then halted in frustration. If he walked in now, they would know he had been eavesdropping. Arabella said, "Josh is in love with you, darling, and wants to marry you."

With a flippancy that grated on Josh's nerves Clem replied, "That's news to me. I don't want to marry anyone, Mother... now how are we going to celebrate your engagement?"

"Tomorrow I shall buy her a ring," Graham announced. "A sapphire to go with your eyes, Arabella. And tonight, if you don't mind, Clem, I'm going to take her to the best restaurant in town for everything from caviar to champagne. A dinner *à deux*."

"Sounds great," Clem said, and Josh wondered if he was the only one to pick up the strain underlying her voice. He began quietly backing toward the front door, and when he reached it, opened it with equal quietness, edging through it and pulling it shut. He had to rescue Clem; she was doing a wonderful job with Graham and Arabella, but he was not sure how much longer she could keep it up.

He crept across the front porch, hoping none of the neighbors were watching him, and then marched back toward the door, whistling one of Handel's more exuberant melodies as he pulled it open and stepped indoors. "Anyone home?" he called.

An hour later, during which every platitude concerning love and marriage seemed to be said at least twice, Graham and Arabella left to go downtown. After waving goodbye from the front door, Clem pulled it shut and said, leaning against the panels and shutting her eyes, "Thank God that's over—I've got a splitting headache."

"You did get bumped on the head with a box only forty-eight hours ago," Josh said.

She opened her eyes; they were as cool and unwelcoming as they had been the first day he had crossed the threshold. "Let's not play games, Josh."

"Okay—why have you got a headache?"

"Because my mother's getting married for the fifth time and because she told me you're in love with me and want to marry me."

He was suddenly glad to have it all out in the open. "I've never been able to fault you for your honesty, Clem," he said with a small smile. "Your relationship with your mother I can't do anything about. But yes, I'm in love with you and I'd like you to marry me."

Her voice sharpened. "Not very diplomatic of you to tell my mother your plans before you saw fit to tell me."

"I don't think I have to tell anyone—it stands out all over me. You're the only one who hasn't seen it."

"And that's because I don't want to," she spat. "You've spoiled everything! Why couldn't we just have had an affair? None of this talk of love and marriage— just the two of us pleasing each other in bed. Because you did please me . . . I loved everything we did."

With the horrible certainty that all his future happiness depended on the next few minutes, Josh said, "I loved being in bed with you because I love you, Clem— I can't separate the two. The reason I didn't share my feelings with you was because I thought you needed time . . . time to get used to making love, time to learn to trust me and your own emotions. For the same reason, I wish Arabella hadn't arrived so soon."

"*You're* the one who invited Graham."

"I'm not going to apologize for that. He and your mother belong together."

"Sure—for how long?"

He held her gaze with his own. "For the rest of their lives. Which is what I want, too—you and I together for the rest of our lives. That's what loving you means to me."

"I can't stand all this heavy-duty emotion," Clem cried wildly. "You can't trust it. I don't care what you say— it doesn't last."

With all the force of his personality Josh said, "Marry me, Clem, and risk that it will."

"I'd have to be crazy to do that!"

"I can't guarantee anything. But I do know that without risk you might as well be dead, and if it's sure solutions you're looking for you'll always be disappointed. I love you, Clem. I'll love you until the day I die, and don't ask me to explain that because I can't. But I know it in my bones—I know you're the woman for me, in my bed, by my side, bearing my children, growing old with me. You're the one I want, and I swear I'll be faithful to you and love you to the best of my ability all the days of my life." He swallowed hard, his eyes boring into hers. "Risk it—because body and soul I'm yours."

She had paled, the anger wiped from her face as if someone had passed a cloth over it. "You terrify me when you talk like that, Josh—I can't do it, I can't!"

He took a step closer, knowing he would not touch her, for that was too crude a weapon in this fight for his life. "You can, I know you can. You're a woman of passion and courage and honesty... I know it."

She shook her head, saying in a choked voice, "You've blinded yourself to the real me—you're only seeing what you want to see. I can't marry you; I'm afraid to. You've got to believe me, because it's the truth."

She had always been honest with him. Josh felt the world lurch beneath his feet and said harshly, "No...no, it can't be the truth, Clem."

She was almost crying, her body taut with her effort to convince him. "It *is* the truth. I'm sorry, I'm truly sorry, I didn't mean to hurt you."

She meant it. He had lost. He felt a vast emptiness open inside him, an emptiness that when it reached its limits would dissolve into inchoate pain; he had to get out of here before that happened. With a blind gesture he reached for the door. "Josh!" she said sharply. "Are you all right? Where are you going?"

He had no idea. He only knew he could not physically bear being in the same room with her for one minute longer. Marshaling all his will-power, he said in a voice that seemed to come from somewhere outside him, "It's okay, I'm just going out for a while, I'll be back later."

"You shouldn't drive——"

"It's okay," he repeated, and blundered past her.

He took the steps one by one; the rain appeared to have stopped. He got in his car, managed to get the key in the ignition and started the engine. He still had no idea where he was going, but he could not stay here within sight of the house that had promised him healing and the woman who, only days ago, had made him happier than he had ever been in his life.

Looking both ways Josh backed out of the driveway and drove down the street. Automatic pilot, he thought blankly, watching his hands and feet do all the correct things, his eyes instinctively keeping track of traffic and pedestrians. Without consciously having made a decision, still driving with immense care, he headed out of the city.

Two hours later he pulled up on the flat rocks near the beach where they had come on Sunday. He got out of the car, his feet sinking in the sand as he crossed the dunes, the marram grass whipping at his ankles. Between the clouds the sun was sinking into the sea in a blaze of orange and gold, and the waves that washed up on the wet sand were painted with the same fiery colors. The beach was deserted except for the herring gulls crying mournfully overhead. He began to walk, and again he had no idea where he was going.

Hands in his pockets, his back to the sunset, Josh marched along the sand in a dead straight line, and sometimes the waves washed over his feet and without even noticing them he still kept walking. He was not thinking about anything; he was incapable of thought. His whole body was a sea of pain from which waves surged over him, drowning him, and the waves said that Clem did not love him, that Clem would not marry him, that he had lost and was more alone than he had ever been in the dark hole of the prison.

Behind his back the sun was swallowed by the sea. Overhead flocks of gulls, now silent, flew offshore to an island to roost, their sleek bodies black against the fading sky. The ocean changed from orange to slate to black, black as Clem's dress; the foam was chalk-white, bone-white on the dark sand.

The wind ruffled Josh's hair; at some dim level he was aware of being cold, of gooseflesh on his bare arms, for he was wearing only a short-sleeved shirt. He hunched his shoulders, vaguely looking around him.

He was at the far end of the beach, where tumbled rocks lank with seaweed led to cliffs fragrant with juniper and close-knit spruce trees. The sand had run out. Stars twinkled coldly in the sky.

Still without thought, he found a boulder and sat down on it, bringing his knees to his chin for protection against the wind, which was knifing through him like an April wind, like the wind the first day he had gone to Clem's. *Clem*...

Agony ripped through him. He buried his face in his knees and sat very still, waiting for it to subside, wishing he didn't feel so cold. It somehow didn't seem appropriate that he should be concerned about the temperature when his heart was broken.

The waves hissed on the beach, and gurgled in retreat. A branch creaked from the woods at his back. The other noise he could hear, Josh realized with faint surprise, was the chattering of his teeth. He clenched them together, and found that he was shivering in violent spasms, and that no matter how hard he tried he could not stop the rattling of one jaw against the other. He felt cold to the bone, so cold that he would never be warm again...maybe this was what death was like, he thought numbly. Cold so intense that all the warmth of life was eradicated. Hell was ice, not fire...

He would have given his soul for a sweater. No, he thought in confusion, it was Clem he would have given his soul for.

And then, like a signal, he felt the first fierce flush of heat and the stab of pain in his forehead. He raised his head, staring blindly at the serried black waves.

You fool, Josh...it's malaria. You might have a broken heart but you're also having an attack of malaria. And all your drugs are in your bedroom in Clem's house.

He brought a hand to his face, which was burning hot. His pulse was bounding and he suddenly realized he was agonizingly thirsty. In the prison they had once left him without water for two full days...

He was not in the prison now. He was free, free to walk back to his car and go for help. He had had more than one attack of malaria, and they were not fatal; all he had to do was find someone to take him home. He slid his feet to the sand and pushed himself upright, and nearly cried out loud from the ringing in his ears and the lancing pain in his head. Staggering like a drunken man, he began walking back the way he had come.

Twice Josh had to crouch by the water's edge while he lost what felt like every morsel of food he had ever eaten, and each time he had to fight against the temptation to slake his raging thirst in the ice cold water of the sea. But each time he managed to lever himself upright; the harsh panting he could hear was his own breathing, the wavering footprints in the sand were also his own. His body felt as though it were on fire, burning endlessly. Hell is fire, not ice...

Halfway down the beach his knees gave out. He sank down onto the wet sand, which felt deliciously cool against his heated skin. A wave washed over his legs, and the water was chill and wet; it would put out the fire that seemed to be raging through his body, he thought dimly. He rested his cheek on the sand and closed his eyes.

The retreating tide left him there, stranded on the beach like a piece of flotsam.

When Josh woke up, his first sensation was that it was raining, for water was dripping onto his hand and wrist. But only on his hand; and anyway, he was flat on his back in a bed. Frowning to himself as he tried to puzzle this out, he opened his eyes. There was a ceiling above his head, a white ceiling, newly painted.

"Josh!" Clem gasped. "Oh, Josh, you're awake."

She was not in bed with him. Turning his head, which seemed to take an immense effort, he saw that she was sitting beside the bed and that she was crying, her tears falling on the hand she had cradled in her own. The walls were also white, and the bed was institutional; he was in a hospital.

And then memory came pouring back. She had turned him down. He had driven to the beach. He had had an attack of malaria. He pulled his hand free and said roughly, "How did I get here? Where is it anyway?"

Clem scrubbed at her face with her hand; she was wearing an old shirt in an unbecoming shade of mauve and his heart turned over with love for her. Love she did not want. He snarled, "I don't know what the hell you're doing here."

She sat up straight, a faint flush of pink touching her pale cheeks. "A couple from Lunenburg went for a walk on the beach in the middle of the night and their dog found you lying on the sand. They got you to the nearest hospital, and the doctor phoned me... your address was on your driver's license. Arabella and Graham are out in the hall. I'm here because I love you."

Knowing he could not have heard her rightly, feeling at a distinct disadvantage lying flat on his back, Josh hauled himself up on one elbow and retorted, "Don't try and make a fool out of me, Clem. You don't love me—you went to great pains last night to convince me that you don't, and that you never would."

The pink patches in her cheeks spread. She said vigorously, not sounding at all loverlike. "I changed my mind." Then, her head to one side, her eyes narrowed, she went on, "Well, no, that's not really it. I guess what I did was discover my own mind. Realize what I'd known all along but had refused to admit... maybe I've known it ever since I was ten."

His pulse seemed to be pounding again in a way he was sure the medical profession would not approve, and his head felt as light as air. Quelling the surge of hope that had lanced through him, Josh said scornfully, "Come off it—so what if you do love me? You're too scared to marry me, you said you were."

"You're not being very helpful!" Clem said crossly.

"Why should I be? I had the worst night of my life because of you, and I've had a few bad ones to compare it with." His voice rose. "I love you, and even now when I don't have the strength of one of Major's kittens I want to haul you down in the bed and make love to you. But I won't make love to you if you're going to keep on dating guys like Manuel!"

"I changed my mind on that, too," she said.

He scowled at her. "What do you mean?"

She put a hand on his chest and pushed him back against the pillows. "Lie down, you look dreadful. I'm trying to tell you that I've done a lot of growing up in the last twelve hours. I felt terrible after you left, just terrible, and then, when Graham and my mother came home, Mother and I had a blazing fight." She bit her lip, her face an entrancing mixture of shame and amusement. "We yelled at each other, we said things that have been buried for years, and then all of sudden we were in each other's arms and crying our heads off and saying how much we loved each other—it was quite a scene."

Josh adjusted the pillow under his head, his eyes trained on Clem's face. He could imagine the scene all too clearly; hope burgeoned in his breast again and it was an effort to keep his features under control. "Where was Dad while all this was going on?"

"Very wisely keeping out of the way." Clem leaned forward, her face vivid with emotion. "I've been angry with Mother for years, but last night was the first time I confronted that anger. I feel—lighter, Josh, as though without knowing it I've been carrying a burden all this time, that's been weighing me down and stopping me from being myself." Her brows wrinkled. "It's amazing what a good fight will do."

He said deliberately, "When we're married, I expect we'll have a few."

"I expect we——" She broke off, biting her lip. "You mean after last night you'll still marry me?"

His smile broke through. "I talked a lot about risk last night, didn't I?"

Clem sat up straight; beneath the laughter in her gray eyes uncertainty still lingered. "Under the circumstances I certainly don't expect you to get down on your knees—but I would like a formal proposal of marriage."

Josh sat up in bed, grasping her hands in his and said, "Clem, dearest Clem, I love you—will you marry me?"

Clem fell against his chest, letting out her breath in a huge sob. The door swung open and a white-jacketed doctor walked into the room followed by three interns. Josh said forcefully, "Come back in five minutes . . . she hasn't said yes yet."

"Of course I will," Clem wept.

The doctor said forbearingly, "We'll give you half an hour, Mr. MacNeill, before we come back. But you're the first case of malaria in this hospital, an excellent opportunity for the medical staff to observe a fortunately very rare disease." Then his eyes twinkled. "Good luck."

The door closed to a tactful slit. Josh said, "Oh, God, Clem, I love you. Come here."

Wiping her eyes, she scrambled up on the starched white spread. "I've cried more in the last few hours than in my entire life," she muttered. "Josh, I'm sorry I sent you away last night, more sorry than I can say. You were right all along, I was running and I wasn't seeing how much Mother has changed, and it took you to shake me up and make me realize what a constricted life I was leading—a life based on fear. Fear of involvement, fear of commitment." She burrowed her cheek into his chest. "I can't believe I'm actually here with you, saying all this."

"Let's see if I can convince you," Josh said huskily, and raised her face to his.

After an indeterminate length of time, during which Josh discovered he was not nearly as weak as he had thought he was, Clem said, "I *do* want to marry you—and I think three children is a nice number, don't you?"

"Perfect," he said, and kissed her again.

After another long pause she mumbled, "I was so frightened last night. I knew something was wrong when you weren't home by midnight, but I hadn't got a clue what to do or where to start looking for you...it was awful. And then when the hospital phoned, for a split second I thought you were dead. That's when I knew for sure that I loved you and that the risk of loving you was nothing like the risk of losing you."

He drew her closer into his arms. "It wasn't a great night for either of us, was it?" He nuzzled into her neck. "We could have a double wedding, along with Dad and Arabella."

She chuckled. "I don't think they'll want to wait for us."

"I don't want to wait, either," Josh said, and set about proving to her just how impatient he was.

When he finally released her, Clem said breathlessly, "The doctors won't know what to make of your heart rate."

"It'll give them a whole new perspective on malaria," said Josh.

A tap came at the door. Clem slid to the floor and when the procession of interns entered she was sitting beside the bed, her hands folded decorously in her lap. The doctor, who had two married daughters and a married son, ignored both her flushed cheeks and Josh's heart rate, and soon pronounced Josh fit enough to be discharged. "Take it easy for the next couple of days," he advised.

But after lunch Arabella and Graham went out to make arrangements for a special license, and Clem let it be known that she had been given the whole day off work. So in the bed upstairs, with Major's kittens mewling in the background and to the satisfaction of both Clem and himself, Josh very thoroughly ignored the doctor's advice.